A VERY NATURAL THING

SUZI HUEBSCH

FOR EVERYONE
EVERYWHERE:

MAY YOU GET WHAT YOU WANT,
AND STILL WANT IT ONCE YOU GET
IT

1

We are all ignorant of our earliest years. Our parents, aunts and uncles tell of who we were, or at least what we were like, when we were infants and toddlers. Maybe they tell us about when we too young to care for ourselves and relied on them because they hope we will return the favor when they get too old to look after themselves.

I knew zero about myself until I was about seven years old, living in Sundown, a patch of nothing several hours away from the big Canadian city of Bayporte. Sundown's only thing to brag about was the big factory where they made Goofies, the candy everyone loved. The air was laden with the smell of sugar and chocolate. One of the dirty faced local boys was Broderick Dillard; we called him Brick for short. One day, during the walk home from school, he said, "Darcie, I gotta take a piss. Wanna watch?"

I shrugged. "Yeah, sure."

He hauled out his dingus and I said, "Why is there all that skin hanging around it?"

"I was born that way. All boys are. If my mum didn't like it, she could have taken me to the doctor and have it cut off."

"But your mum liked it."

"I guess so."

"Well, I'm glad I have nothing down there to cut

off. I'm lucky that way."

"In a few years you're gonna get titties, and one day you might get them cut off. That's what happened to my auntie."

"I'm not gonna get titties."

"Sure you will. You'll get big ugly titties that flop around. All women get 'em."

"You shut up or I'll kick your balls up through the roof of your mouth," I told him.

"I'll shut up," he said, "if you promise not to tell anyone that I showed you my dick."

I laughed. "Oh, I won't tell. There's nothing to tell, anyway. It's just an ugly wrinkled thing that isn't worth looking at or talking about."

"It's not ugly. It's a thing of beauty. See how big it is? It hangs down to my knees."

"It's too big. It's ugly. My cousin Roy has one but it's not nearly as big as yours. I bet we could make some money off it."

"How would we make money off my Johnson?"

"After school we can take some of the kids back here and let them look at it. Charge them a quarter each. Four gawkers would mean one dollars. It adds up fast, you know."

He shook his head. "I'm not standing there with it hangin' out so's people can laugh at me."

"Let them laugh all they want, so long as they pay their money first."

The next day at school, I gathered up some kids at recess and told them about Sundown's newest attraction. Brick kept quiet, and for much of the day I feared he would lose his nerve, but he didn't. Right after school, I led a dozen of our classmates out to a section of the woods between the school and the grocery store, and when we were sure no adult was within half a mile, Brick dropped trou and let our customers check him out. He sort of blushed at first, but then his vanity won over and he beamed with pride as the girls stared for the longest time, then shrieked with disgust and pleasure at the sight of his oversized whang and scrotum. He kept the show going until the red-faced kids looked from his junk to each other, then shrugged and decided they had seen enough. He and I were three dollars richer, and that was the most money either of us had had, ever.

Kids being kids, they went to school the next day and told others about Brick the human tripod. For a week and a half or so, we had a highly lucrative business. I even bought a few boxes of Goofies and handed handfuls of candies to our audience. Sharing Goofies was a good way of making friends. My cousin Roy tried to put himself on display, too, but he lacked Brick's endowment and got few takers. I felt sorry for him and shared gave him some of my profits.

Cay Nanceford came by each day to look at Brick. She also seemed to be the last one to leave. Cay was all bright red hair and light green eyes. She let out a huge squeal as soon as his Levi's collapsed to his knees. One time she asked if she could touch his privates. Foolishly, he nodded yes; she reached over and gave his pecker a hard yank and screamed in naughty jubilation.

"Let go, Cay," I said. "That's his, not yours. Plus, it has to last him the rest of his life." She released his penis and skulked away. I said, "Brick, why did you let her do that for free? If you're going to let them touch you, at least charge extra for it. Or at least charge the other kids extra but let Cay play with it all she wants after everyone else goes home."

Brick shrugged. "If you say so."

So we charged extra for touching, and made more money than ever until Strom Earle snitched us off to Miz Cleaver, one of our teachers. First she called Reenie, and then phoned Brick's mum. Miz Cleaver said, "I've heard nasty things about Brick and Darcie's afterschool activities in the woods."

When I got home that night, I had scarcely gotten through the front door when I heard Reenie bellow, "Darcie! Come in here!"

"Yes, Mum."

"I got a call from someone sayin' you've been out in the woods with Brick Dillard's willie. Don't lie to me—Strom told Miz Cleaver that you're out there just about every day."

"No, Mum, I'm never played with Brick's you-know-what." Which, strictly speaking, was absolutely true.

"Quit lyin', you mouthy little brat. I know you've been beatin' him off out there in front of all the other brats in Sundown."

"No, Mum! I swear to God! I've never put my hands anywhere near him! And I never would!" I knew the pointlessness of telling her that I was his business manager; she would have considered that worse than being his sex-show partner. Anyway, in her view, to be a child was to be a liar.

"You've made a fool of me in front of everyone in Sundown, and I feel like throwin' you out of this house right now. You and your hoity-toity ways, blowin' in and out of this house whenever you please. You keep your nose in those books, learnin' those fancy words and throwin' them around like you're better'n me and everyone else. You're the last one on Earth who oughta have an attitude. Miss Lady, out there in the woods, fiddlin' with his big dink. Well, you wanna know somethin', you little bitch? You think you're no fine and smart, but you're really not. You should be the humblest thing around, and you wanna know why? It's because you aren't mine, and I don't want you around here anymore, now that I know your game, what you're about. I'll tell you who you are: You're Sals Lingersoll's bastard child, that's who. Now let's see how hoity-toity you are!"

I frowned. "Who's Sals Lingersoll?"

"Oh, just the trampiest, filthiest excuse for a whore that ever lived in Sundown. That's right—she was your natural mother."

"Well, what of it? Doesn't matter to me. The only thing that matters is that I'm me and I'm here now."

"Oh, I'd say it matters plenty that you are a bastard child. Those that are born in wedlock are blessed by the Lord. Those who are not are cursed."

"I don't believe it. Anyway, even if it's true, I don't care."

"Well, you *should* care, you dumbass. It's just your soul we're talkin' about. As you go through life, just see how far your snobbish ways and bookish talk get you once people figure out you're a bastard. You act like one, too. Someone says, 'Daricie's been out in the woods jackin' off Brick Dillard,' and all I can think is, 'Darcie's just like her mum. Sals woulda done just the same thing.'"

Reenie paused to take a breath. Her face had gone so red that I feared she might drop dead from a stroke. She looked at her trembling hands, then clamped them onto my shoulders and shook me hard. "Snooty little bitch! Bastard! I took you in, gave you a home and saved you from life in that orphanage! You thank me by actin' like you're better than me, then you go out into the woods and do what you did. You better git your shit together or I'll throw your ass into the gutter. Hear me?"

I grabbed her hands and wrenched them from my shoulders. "Get your hands off me! If you're not my mum and I'm just some tramp you took in, get your fucking hands off me!" I scrambled out the door and raced through the wheat fields up to the woods. The sun had mostly disappeared; the sky held only the tiniest tinge of rose.

O.K., I thought, so I'm a bastard. How does that make me different from—or worse than—everyone else? Is Reenie just trying to scare me? She's always been trying to control me through fear. If she's all hung up on this bastard thing, too bad for her, and too bad for the rest of Sundown if they hate illegitimate children, too. To hell with Brick Dillard and his big ugly prick. He got me into this predicament, and just when we were starting to generate some serious income, it has to come crashing down. I'm going to wait till I catch Strom Earle alone, and when I do—lights out, man! Then Mum will find out and she'll rag all over me about it. Who else knows I'm a bastard? I'll bet that Big Mouth Annie knows, and if so, she's told everyone else. Well, I'm not going back into that house and face those people now. I'm going to camp out in these endless Canadian woods and wait till Strom Earle comes around, then I'm going to whip his ass. I wonder if Brick's mum has laid into him about exposing himself for money, and did he admit it? Did he mention me? I hope not. Brick knows his dick is big and that people will pay to see it. Maybe he'll be able to make a career of showing it off. I wonder if the other Sundown kids know my personal business. I can tolerate having Big Mouth Annie and Mum know I'm a bastard but not anyone else. If it matters to people, then those people don't matter. I'm not sure why it's such a big deal. I mean, I'm the illegitimate one and I'm O.K. with it, so why shouldn't the rest of the world feel that way? Ol' Mum sure got hot about it. I hadn't seen her that mad in a long time. It hurts her very, very deeply that I am a bastard. Myself, I figure that I got myself from the womb to where I am now, and that's the main thing. But Mum just threw it in my face, said, 'You're a bastard, and that bothers me a lot and I'm going to use it against you from now on,' so I don't exactly have the option of going back there. I remember how Mum kept reminding me of the time I kicked my grandmother in the butt when I was five years old. Yessir, I'm staying in the woods indefinitely; I can live on nuts and berries and rabbits, too. If necessary, I won't eat anything and I'll starve to death out here. At some point the search party will find me, bring me back to Mum and she'll be wracked with guilt for the rest of her life. She called my birth mother all those awful names; I wonder what that woman looked like. I look nothing at all like Mum, Dad or anyone else around here. I'm dark, with thick black hair, big dark eyes and pink lips. I wonder if my birth mother ever regrets giving me up so that the Rotas could raise me. Did I do something to offend her when I was born? I'll never know; but I do know that she would have been deeply offended by my decision to sell tickets for viewings of Brick's dick. Yeah, that was pretty despicable behavior. Maybe I did that because Reenie Rota raised me wrong. I'll blame it all on her. I wish she would keel over and die.

The woods got very dark very fast. It got cold, too, and I couldn't find anything to eat. I started to shiver from cold and hunger. I resolved to return to the house and bide my time till I was old enough to get a job, then I'd skedaddle forever. I groped my way back home and let myself in. Nobody said anything to me; everyone had gone to bed.

2

Roy, my cousin, was eleven—my age and height—but he was fat and I was thin. Eddie, Roy's brother, was thirteen and already sounded like an adult. He worked down at the gas station, so Roy and I had to go picking potatoes.

"Darcie," he said, "this is boring. Let's go to the store and get a pop."

I nodded. "But we'll have to go down by the gully and hide behind the wrecked tractor or my mum will see us. She'll shit if she sees us drinking pop when we're supposed to be working."

We stopped our thankless task and hustled out to Missus Hurd's minuscule grocery store with its ancient Coke sign flapping over the door.

"Well, hello Darcie and Roy!" Missus Hurd called out. "Been out helping your mum, eh?"

"Yes, ma'am," said Roy. "We've been out pickin' potatoes and it's just ever such fun."

"I guess you're thirsty," she said. "How would you each like a nice cold Coke?"

We nodded with the profoundest eagerness. As

we exited the store, we saw Beatrice Sputz approaching.

"Hey, Beatrice, where ya goin'?"

"To the store," she mumbled. She was Jewish and Reenie was forever admonishing me to stay away from that kid. I needed no admonition. Everyone avoided Beatrice Sputz because she always had her hand in her pants as if her crotch were covered with mosquito bites. Worse, she stank. For the longest time, I believed that being Jewish meant that a person showered too seldom and scratched herself all the time.

"Beatrice," I said, "have you seen Strom Earle today?"

"Yeah, he's down by the pond."

"You see him, you tell him that Roy has a surprise for him."

"O.K., I'll do that." Beatrice hurried away, eager to deliver my message to Strom.

Roy smirked. "I'm afraid to ask what kind of present you have in mind for Strom."

I smirked back. "You'll like it. He won't."

We went into the woods and I collected a dozen rabbit droppings. "What you going to do with those?" Roy asked.

"Something fun." I went back into the store, bought a box of raisins, gobbled up half of them and dumped the feces into the box. We went near the pond and spotted Strom. "Don't say anything. Just watch and enjoy." I hurried over to where Strom sat with a stick and string, fishing the empty water. I thought he was the dumbest kid around in a valley full of dummies. He'd made it through Grade 4 by kissing the teacher's ass. Now we were in Grade 6 and he remained illiterate and innumerate. Big Mouth Annie said that Strom's family was too big so none of them got enough to eat and Strom's brain was deprived of protein. I cared very little about his stupidity; all I knew was that I despised him. At school, he played the snitch whenever he saw me breaking the rules, which was very often.

Strom looked up and saw me. I saw his face go white with panic, as if he didn't know whether to run, shit or stay put.

"Hey, Strom," I said with a smile, "you getting any bites?"

He shook his head. "Not yet."

"Strom," I said, sitting down next to him, "I've been thinking. We've been enemies for too long. You snitch me off and I beat the shit out of you, right? Well, maybe there's a better way. Maybe we could just shake hands and be friends."

Strom beamed. "Yeah, Darcie! I would love to be your friend!"

"Sounds good. Here, I have a little something for you. A peace offering. I know you love raisins, so I bought this box just for you."

I handed him the box, and he downed its contents in one gulp. Then Roy bounded down to join us. He sat next to me and giggled. I elbowed him in the ribs.

Strom said, "You guys are lookin' at each other funny. What's the deal?"

I told him, and his face fell. "You didn't do that, Darcie. Please tell me you didn't."

"Damn right I did, you freakin' snitch. You get me into trouble once more and I'll get you to do much worse than eat rabbit shit."

Strom looked down at the empty red box and

swallowed hard. I expected him to vomit at any moment. I got up and so did Roy. We ran off towards my home, and he burst out laughing, holding his sides, scarcely able to keep moving. I looked back towards the pond and saw Strom curled up in the fetal position. He was probably shuddering, and maybe crying, too. *That's what happens when you mess with me, sucker*, I thought. Then: *If I punished him that well, how come I'm not feeling that good about it?*

"He learned his lesson, Darcie. You taught him right from wrong," said Roy.

"Just be quiet, will you?"

Roy looked me up and down, smiling, then shrugged. "We've had our fun for the day. Let's get back before Reenie and Big Mouth Annie come lookin' for us."

3

The summer of getting back at Strom Earle was also the summer when most of our crops dried up and Jeri died. She was Roy's birth mum, a tall, thin, mostly quiet woman. I called her Auntie even though she was of no relation to me. Of course, nobody there was related to me; I was dark and exotic, as if I had been flown in from the other side of the world, and they were mainly pale, freckled Canadians. That summer was memorable for all the wrong reasons, and the bad stuff started off with Gib's being threatened with a knife.

A few days after I humiliated Strom, Gib—Jeri's husband—came into their house all bloody. Jeri screamed at the sight of him, and Annie went right away for a bowl of cold water to rinse his wounds. Roy, Eddie and I were there, plus Jeri and Annie. As the women cleaned him up, Jeri said, "Gib, did you go and lose your temper again? Fighting doesn't resolve anything, you know."

Gib sighed once or twice and seemed to relax a bit. "Yes, I lost my temper. But I didn't have a drink. Nothing."

Annie frowned at him but kept up her ministrations. Leroy, Gib's son, stood over his father and said, "Did you get him good, Dad? Did you get him good?"

"Roy," said Jeri, "I wish you wouldn't seem so pleased that your father got into a fight." She looked old and tired and afraid; violence was one of those things that freaked her out. She refused to watch the TV news because she couldn't bear all the killing. Jeri was pregnant; her due date was just a couple of weeks away, and Reenie muttered something about this being an unwanted baby.

"So," Jeri said to Gib, "what was it about *this* time?"

Gib said, "This time it was about our boys. That asshole Clark comes in today and brags to me that his son just got an appointment to the Canadian Naval Academy. He says, 'And how are *your* boys doin'?' I said, 'Well, I s'pose Roy and Eddie are goin' to the Academy, too, when it's time. I served in the military, so there shouldn't be any problem with gettin' my boys in.' So Clark just stands there and laughs. He says, 'Bein' a veteran don't mean shit when it comes to gettin' into the Academy. Anyway, everyone in Sundown knows you got two of the dumbest boys in the whole valley.' Well, I said, 'Nobody speaks to *me* that way!' so I punched his ass out. Only he got back up, took out his switchblade and, well, here I am."

"Yeah, here you are," said Annie, shaking her head. "Maybe next time you won't make it home. You keep this up and the cops will come by and take you away. Was old Clark still breathin' when you left him?"

"Yes he was. Wish I could say his face was as blue as the sky and his tongue was hangin' out of his mouth. Burl came by the shop on his way home and busted it up. He's down there with Clark now, tryin' to put things right. Burl, he's so good-natured, he can get just about everyone to smile and shake hands. He sent me home 'cause I was bleedin' all over the floor."

Jeri paused to check on dinner. Gib said, "Sweetie, our boys aren't stupid, are they? You just wait—they'll find themselves and do some good. When that happens, it'll make me feel much better than I've ever felt punchin' out Clark."

She smiled. "Oh, I'm sure they'll figure out where they belong in this world, and they'll do just fine. In the meantime, I don't think that punchin' out Clark is showin' them the best way to manage anger."

Burl came in and tossed his cap a dozen feet onto the nearest hook. We all cheered and he bowed a bit. He held a greasy parcel of butcher's paper. "I got lamb tonight. They had it left over, so we're havin' stew tonight. Break out the onions and carrots."

I came over and gave him a hug. "I *love* lamb stew, Daddy." He said to Gib, "I wonder how they other guy looks." Gib looked up and grinned. Even though Burl was maybe a decade older than Gib, Gib often treated him the way a boy treats his dad.

Reenie and Jeri were fine cooks. "Clear away the rags and bloody water," Reenie said, "'cause we're about to cook lamb stew." Presently they brought a boiling pot of delicious-smelling stew to the table. Roy and I sat next to Burl, while Jeri and Gib sat across from each other. Annie yakked away about this and that—she seemed *so* much in love with the sound of her own voice!—and Burl talked, too. He said mean and funny things about Kaj, the big guy who ran the butcher's shop, and everyone laughed at his observations. Burl followed the news and made fun of the prime minister of Canada. At school, the teachers said that the prime minister was a very special man who deserved everyone's respect, but Burl said that the prime minister had a job where, no matter what he did, many people would criticize him, and so part of being the prime minister was being laughed at and mocked. I decided then that I didn't want to become the prime minister, ever.

Soon thereafter, Jeri went off to Valley General Hospital to have her baby. I didn't really understand what was going on, except that her baby—named Burl, in honor of my father—died almost right away. Jeri didn't come home. I crept around one evening and eavesdropped on Annie, Reenie and Gib as they sat on the back steps. That was where they did most of their serious talking. Roy came along, too, so we both hung way back and strained to listen.

Gib's voice sounded hoarse, as if he'd been talking nonstop for a month. "Reenie, Jeri didn't say a word about bein' in pain. I figured all ladies feel poorly when they're in a family way, but I didn't know it was worse than that. If she'd said somethin', I would have got her to a doctor."

Annie said, "Gibby, don't blame yourself for any of this. Jeri was my daughter, so I knew her about as well as anyone could. She didn't complain, and she thought doctors charged you an arm and a leg just to say hello. She thought that she was feelin' bad because of her pregnancy and that she would feel fine again soon enough."

Gib sighed. "I was her husband. She was my wife. She should have told me. I was supposed to know about these things."

Reenie said, "Women have ailments they don't tell their men about. Jeri kept things to herself. I don't know if she herself knew she had cancer everywhere. Anyway, she's not dead yet."

"Just a matter of time," said Gib.

"I hope it happens soon," said Annie. "I hate to see her suffer. God will take her soon. It has nothing to do with us. It is up to Him now." Simple as that. God was the Boss; if He wanted her, well, it was a done deal.

"Amen to that," said Reenie.

Roy grabbed my arm and whispered, "Darcie, why are they talkin' about my mom like that? She's O.K., right? She comin' home soon?"

"I don't know, Roy. Sounds like Aunt Jeri's going to die." I felt a catch in my throat and a tear trickle down my cheek. I hated to cry; I wanted the world to think I was the toughest chick alive, never feeling a moment of weakness. I squeezed Roy's hand and whispered, "We weren't supposed to hear them. Let's pretend we don't know anything. Who knows? Maybe the doctors are wrong and your mom will be fine. Good things happen sometimes." My words failed to assuage his grief. Roy shut his eyes and tears streamed out. I led him out to the cornfield so the adults wouldn't hear him. "I don't wanna lose my mum," he cried out. He wept until exhaustion set in and then he fell asleep. Presently Reenie called out into the darkness for us to come in, so I pulled Roy to his feet and half-carried his fat, aggrieved body into the house and put him on his lumpy little bed. Roy slept in the same room as Eddie, and I slept with Reenie and Burl in my own bed. Many times, I would have preferred to be in there with Roy, especially when he was so upset, but people insisted it was inappropriate. "Mum," I said, "please let me stay in here with Roy, just for tonight. O.K.?"

She shook her head. "You're not sleepin' with them boys. Eddie's mostly a man now. You sleep where you belong. You'll understand when you're older." Roy must have told Eddie what he knew because the next day Eddie was all hangdog, looking sullen and saying little.

The following week, Jeri died. The entire population of Sundown attended her funeral; people smiled and pointed at all the beautiful flowers. Gib just about bankrupted himself when he bought the casket. "She loved nice things," he explained. "Forever is a long time, so she should have a comfy place to rest." Annie handled all of the arrangements and whatnot by herself; she wanted no assistance whatsoever from Roy and me, and we felt better than fine about that. All the people turned out in their Sunday best to say goodbye to someone who had already left. Reenie made me wear a dress that itched me all over, and I felt worse than the cadaver. The preacher said blah-blah-blah about what a lovely person Jeri had been, but then he forgot about her and went on about the beauty of heaven as if it were an actual place, like Hawaii on a perfect day but a zillion times better. When they finally lowered the fancy box into the humble Sundown ground, Annie whimpered and said, "My little girl's gone." She fell backwards, but Burl grabbed her and held her upright. Gib held Roy and Eddie's hands and remained absolutely motionless. He just stared straight into that rectangular, six-foot-deep hole and stayed mute. I watched Roy's face contort and relax, then contort again, as if he were trying not to bawl. His stubborn cowlick stood straight up, so I stared at it with all my energy so that I wouldn't burst into tears and blow my image as the toughest chick around.

After the funeral everyone went back to the house. Neighbors and relatives from throughout the valley came by with food even though nobody felt much like eating. Gib greeted everyone with a quiet dignity and Annie accepted huge and good wishes with the exuberance of one who truly craves attention even when it's at the funeral of her daughter.

As soon as dusk arrived, the guests cleared out and we were left to deal with each other, ourselves and our loss. Reenie set the table, saying, "You kids need to get some grub up in you."

"I don't want to eat," I said. "I have no appetite." I pushed my food around the plate and took tiny bites. After a while, Reenie took away the plates and we kids went off to bed. To Roy and Eddie, I said, "Goodnight, you guys. Tomorrow maybe we should go down to the pond. Go exploring or something."

Eddie nodded. He looked like a middle-aged man who had already seen more than enough of life. "My boss said I don't have to work tomorrow because of Mum." Roy lay in bed crying. "I want my mum back. The preacher said He took her off to a better place. I don't believe it. I want Him to bring my mum back." Reenie came into the room and sat on his bed, holding him. She gave him that tired old rap about how God does what needs to be done and we don't understand Him and His ways because we are only human and humans can't be expected to understand the mind of God.

"Come on, Darcie," she said. "Let's go now so the boys can get some sleep." I nodded and shrugged at Roy, then gave Eddie a little wave. I crawled into my bed and lay staring up at the ceiling, thinking about Auntie Jeri in that box. What would happen if she opened her eyes and figured out she'd been buried alive? How does anyone know that the dead don't suddenly come back to life? The people who are alive don't know shit about being dead. Was Auntie Jeri going to rot in that box and be eaten by bugs? Why did we insist on burying her? She was still young; couldn't we have donated her organs to people who were still alive?

'Well,' I said to myself, 'I'm just not going to lay down in a box and let bugs eat me, because I'm not going to die. I'm going to stay awake and alive. Starting right now. I'm going to go outside and lay down and stare at the stars till the sun comes up.' I got out of bed, tiptoed through down the hall and stopped.

I turned to my right and stared as Burl held Gib and stroked his hair as Gib wailed and shuddered. The two men were muttering to each other, but I couldn't hear much of it. I think Burl kept saying something like 'Hang in there, buddy. You can do it.' I wanted to ask them about it but lost my nerve and hurried back to bed. I had never seen men cry or show each other such tenderness. I didn't think they did such things. But then I guessed that Gib cried like that because he needed to do so, and Burl held him and stroked his hair because that's what Burl needed to do for him. But that was all just one big maybe. I didn't understand it and it disturbed me.

The next morning, the sky was dark gray and rain came down in torrents. We had to stay indoors and wait for the rain to stop. Once it did, the sky stayed dark but a wonderful rainbow appeared. Roy said, "I bet if you went to the end of that rainbow you wouldn't find a pot of gold."

"Doesn't matter. The rainbow alone is enough."

4

Gloria Speer lived on the other side of the pond. Her father sold cars and trucks, and most of us in the valley bought ours from him, so he had more money than anyone else. She wore skirts and dresses all the time, which I disliked, and she was forever kissing the adults' asses, which I hated even more than her fancy clothes. Reenie thought Gloria looked lovely in her outfits and wondered aloud why I didn't try to look like a store-bought little princess instead of a poor valley kid. Gloria and I had been friends, sort of, since Grade 1 and sometimes we hung out together. Reenie beamed each time I headed out to the Speers' place because that meant I was choosing my friends better and at some point I might start emulating Gloria. Roy often joined me, and Gloria seemed O.K. with having him around, but whenever she pulled out her collection of dolls, he and I beat cheeks out of there.

"Let's play doctor," said Gloria. She decided to make Roy the patient and me the nurse.

"I'm no nurse. I give orders, not take them."

"Girls can't be doctors. Maybe Roy should be the doctor."

"Kiss my ass, Speer. Roy's dumber than dog shit. I'm the smart one, so I get to be the doctor. Doesn't matter that I'm a girl."

"Oh, it matters quite a lot. You just like to

pretend it doesn't."

So I hauled off and punched her out. Once she came to herself, she got up and ran out of the room. she returned with her mum, Sarah, who grabbed me by my sweatshirt and gave me what-for about respecting the rights of others. She said I couldn't hang out Gloria again for a week, and I thought that was no big loss. Roy and I started for home.

"Darcie," he said, "I didn't know you wanted to be a doctor."

"I don't. But I'll be damned if I'm going to let anyone say, 'You can't be a doctor because you're a girl.'" Then, "I don't want to be a doctor because being a doctor isn't so great. I want to be great. I want everyone everywhere to say, 'There's Darcie Rota. Isn't she great?'"

"Really? What are you gonna be great at?"

"You'll find out soon enough."

"Tell me now."

"No…but once I achieve greatness, I'll make sure you get some of the spoils, too."

Roy just shrugged.

As soon as we got home, Reenie started pointing at me and scowling as if I'd killed someone. "I just heard from Sarah Speer. She said you beat up on Gloria! Can't you ever play nice? Can't you at least *pretend* to be a nice young lady? You go over there and beat up on the sweetest child in Sundown. I've tried to bring you up right, but you disgrace me every chance you get. I know you're not mind, and I wonder whose you are, with your temper and lack of respect for others."

Roy's jaw dropped. He certainly wasn't the sharpest tool in the shed, but I could tell he understood Reenie just fine. I could have punched *her* out just then for letting Roy in on that big secret. Usually Big Mouth Annie was the one who disseminated everyone's private business throughout Sundown. I hoped Roy could keep my secret to himself.

"Darcie," Reenie said, "I'm gonna make a lady of you this summer. No more runnin' off an' doin' your own thing. I'm gonna teach you to act right, cook, clean and sew. You don't like it? Too bloody bad."

Roy sat down. "If Darcie stays in, I'm stayin' in, too."

Roy, you're wonderful.

"You'll do as you're told," said Reenie. "You're a boy, so's you'll go out and play like boys are supposed to do. Cookin', cleanin' and sewin'? That's for girls. It's not right for you to learn those things."

"I'll learn 'em anyway. Darcie is my best friend and cousin. If she has to stay inside, I'm gonna stay inside, too."

Reenie didn't get cross with him. Instead, in a very matter-of-fact way, she explained to him about small-town Canadian boys who stayed indoors and learned "girls' work." Presently she had Roy white-faced and fighting back tears. Everyone in Sundown, she assured him, would consider him the laughingstock of the valley. Nobody would play with him, and a bunch of them would probably drag him off to the woods with the warning, "If you're gonna stay inside and act like a girl, we're gonna treat you like a girl."

"Auntie Reenie," he said, "I'll do as you say."

Roy, you're such an asshole.

"Darcie," Reenie said, "your first lesson will be canning. I'm going downstairs to get what we'll need." She headed down the stairs, and I hurried to the door, shut it and turned the lock. As soon as she got back to the stop of the stairs, she knocked and said, "I'm locked out. Open it up."

"Better do it," said Roy. "Elsewise we'll get our asses tanned."

I just shook my head. Roy looked from the door to me, then at the door again. He knew better than to go for the door; I could take his fat ass in two minutes if it came down to a physical struggle.

"Darcie! Let me out of here!"

"Only if you promise to let me be. I want to play with the boys and I don't want to learn cooking and sewing. Promise?"

"I will promise you *nothing*."

"Then you better get comfy in there because you're going to be there for a long time." I grabbed Roy and dragged him out of the house. Nobody was home. Annie had gone to the market, Eddie was at the gas station and Gib and Burl were at work. Nobody could hear Reenie as she pounded on the door and cried out for help. "Darcie," Roy said, "we gotta let her out. She'll freeze to death or somethin'."

I shook my head. "She won't do any such thing. She'll just miss a meal or two and lose some weight. It'll do her some good."

Roy scratched his head. "Say, what did she mean by 'you're not mine'?"

"She's full of shit. She was talking out her ass."

"No, she meant somethin'. I mean, you look nothin' like her or Burl. You don't look nothin' like no one around here. You're so dark and all. Maybe

Reenie and Burl took you in when you were a baby. People do that sometimes."

I sighed. "O.K., Roy, here's the deal. Reenie's right—I'm not hers. Never have been. I was born and had nobody so they took me in. I don't know who my birth mum and dad were and I guess I'll never know. I don't belong to anybody. I just belong to me. But I guess that's all right. Don't you?"

He staggered a bit, as if this news were a weight he could not bear. "I thought we were cousins. I thought we were kin. What *are* we?"

"Friends. But sometimes friends can mean more than family."

"What's that word 'bastard' all about? People say it like it's the worst thing in the world."

"It means that your mum and dad were married when you were born, so you're not a bastard. My mum and dad were not married when I was born, so that means I am a bastard."

Roy rolled his eyes. "Seems to me that being married just means they give you a piece of paper. Your mum and dad didn't have that paper, so they stick the word 'bastard' on you.."

I nodded.

"So if we're not blood, I could marry you. Right?"

"Yeah, when we're sixteen or so."

"Well, when that happens, you an' me are goin' to get married."

"Why bother with that? We're together more than most married couples. Anyway, I'm not marrying you or anyone else."

"Oh, *everyone* gets married. It's just something people do, like get born, pay taxes an' die."

"Not me. Darcie Rota will never marry."

33

"I don't know about you, Darcie. You're just makin' things hard on yourself. You don't wanna get married an' you won't be a nurse when we're playin' doctor. You got to do some of those things in life because everyone expects you to do them."

"Wrong. I don't care if the world likes or dislikes me. Everyone's an idiot, anyway. The only thing that matters to me is that I like myself and respect myself."

Roy hooted. "You're a funny girl, Darcie. You got some peculiar ideas on things. Annie always says you need to stop likin' yourself so much and start likin' others more."

"Annie is an idiot too. Everyone laughs at her because she's got such a big mouth and repeats everything she hears. Far as I'm concerned, you can't be happy in life until you like and respect yourself."

"Darcie, everyone likes and respects themselves."

"Do not. Remember when Reenie started in on you about what would happen to you if you did sissy work and the other boys found out? You respect yourself only when the other boys respect you."

"Let's change the subject. How come people get married?"

"So they can get it on."

He frowned. "Hey? What's that mean?"

"Not sure, but it's what married people do."

"You're the smartest kid I know."

"And don't you forget it." Then, "Let's go back inside and see if Reenie is ready to be more reasonable."

I knocked on the door and said, "Mum, are you ready to come out and have a sane conversation with me?"

"Yes. Let me out of here. I'm gettin' all creeped out."

As soon as I opened the door, she jumped at me and grabbed my throat. Then she punched me in the face, stomach and thigh. When I doubled over, she clasped her hands together and started pounding my back. I remember thinking that Reenie had never impressed me as being much of a scrapper. She was calling me names, too, but I couldn't make out which ones. I heard Roy cry out in terror as he ran away. He didn't try to defend me, even though a couple of good kicks to her big ass would have disabled her enough to stop the beating long enough for him and me to escape. Roy could be such a wimp at times.

She sent me to bed without dinner. I couldn't have eaten anyway; she had pounded me in the mouth so many times that I was too sore and swollen to eat. As soon as everyone came home, she said, "Well, let me tell you about what Darcie did today..." I lay in bed, unable to sleep, and listened as Reenie and Burl ripped into each other. "Reenie, the girl is full of life and full of smarts," he practically shouted. "Smarter than the rest of us put together. We need to respect that. Didn't she start readin' when she was three years old? Yes, she did. She's just a girl, a brainy girl tryin' to grow up in a brainless town among boobs and rubes like us."

"Brains aren't the point," Reenie retorted. "She just don't act like a girl. She runs around with the boys all the time. She climbs trees and whatnot. My job as her mother is to teach her to be a woman, but she won't listen to me. She pays me no mind as I try to teach her the things she needs to get by in this world. I tell her she'll need a husband but she won't

35

get one if she's sassin' the males an' givin' them all kinds of backtalk. She says she don't need a husband. You ever heard such nonsense?"

"She wants to go to college and be someone special."

"College is for boys. They'll be runnin' the world when they get older. Her job is to marry one of them and have his children."

"Darcie," he told her, "is goin' to college."

"Is not."

"You don't like it, too bad. My daughter is goin' to college."

Reenie let out a loud, bitter laugh. "What did you just say? 'My daughter'? Did I hear you right? You got it wrong. She's Sals Lingersoll's bastard, in case you forgot. Now you're sayin' 'My daughter.' You make me laugh sometimes, Burl. 'My daughter.'"

"She may as well be my real daughter. I love her that much."

She laughed again. "'Real daughter.' We shoulda had one instead of takin' in Sals' unwanted rug rat. If we'd have had one of our own, I coulda brought her up to be a fine little lady like Gloria Speer instead of that alley cat sleepin' in the back room. When you say 'my daughter,' you're insultin' yourself."

"Sweetie, you're just gettin' yourself all worked up. Darcie is my daughter just as she is yours. A girl needs parents, and ours has us."

"I am not her mother! I am not her fuckin' mother!" Then, "I did not give birth to that little monster. Annie has given birth and she says it's not the same thing. She knows about this and she says that even if you take them in and raise them, they're really not *yours*. You're a man. You don't know about these things. You don't know about anything."

"Mother, father, birth parent, adoption—what difference does it make? As long as you love 'em and take care of 'em right, well, that's all that matters. Darcie is my daughter and I'm her father. Period. I'm gonna make damn sure that she gets what she wants out of life. I'm gonna make sure she has the chance to do things we never had a chance to do. You want her to stay out here in the valley like us, poor folks out in the boonies, watchin' every dime and complainin' about how rough we got it? You want her to have a life like yours—cookin', cleanin' and slavin' away? She's like a flower in the sunshine, but you're standin' over her, you won't let her absorb the sunshine and grow. You just better back off and let her be, let her do her thing. She'll go to Bayporte or Toronto and go as far as her smarts and ambition will take her. That little girl is nobody's fool. You just wait and see. She has no limits."

"You make me sick, Burl. 'She's nobody's fool. She's got no limits.' So she'll run off to Bayporte or Toronto and start thinkin' she's better than everyone else. Well, she already thinks that way. You want to send her to college in a big city and she'll be so full of herself she'll be ridiculous. She's so ashamed of us that she'll go to college and say her folks are dead. She don't give a shit for no one but Number One, and she'll be that way till she dies. She's such a mean little cunt! She locked me in the cellar till I near about froze! What kind of child does that to the woman who's supposed to be her mother?" She continued, "She's poor country people, whether she likes it or not. If she goes to some fancy college, those people will tell right off that she's a country bumpkin and they'll laugh at her. You have dreams for your *daughter* that just won't come true."

Her cruel emphasis on *daughter* made me cringe.

"Reenie," Burl said, "Darcie is gettin' her college education even if you don't like it. You're not lockin' her in this house an' teachin' her to be a lady if that's not what she wants. If she wants to run all over the valley with Roy and put her foot up Gloria Speer's ass, I say fine. Darcie is gonna decide who she is and what she wants, not you."

"Burl Rota," Reenie said, "I got one thing left to say to you. We never fought until she come to live with us, and our only fights were on account of her. If you coulda give me a baby like you were supposed to, we wouldn't have had to take in someone's bastard and fight over her. You were playin' around and you got a disease so we couldn't have our own. This is all your fault and I'll always blame you for it."

"Darcie is gonna go to college," he said. "I'm not askin' you, I'm tellin' you."

"We'll just see about that." Reenie always needed to have the last word.

5

Bess Lindstrom sat next to me that fall in Grade 6 and Roy sat behind us. Bess was tall and slim, blonde and lovely, shy and dimpled. I spent much of that year trying to make her laugh. Miz Epperson was displeased with my antics but she was a kind old thing who only rarely made me stand outside in the hallway. Such punishment made little difference to me; as soon as Miz Epperson's back was turned, I would do a little dance for Bess. I also made an obscene finger gesture at Roy. But Miz Epperson turned towards me at just the wrong moment, saw me give Roy the bird, and said, "Darcie, clearly you love performing, so I'm going to make you the stat of our Christmas play. It will be a Nativity play and you will be the Virgin Mary."

Gloria Speer's face went red. She jumped up and said, "Miz Epperson, that part should be played by a good girl and Darcie is the last girl who should get to play that part."

"Gloria," said our teacher, "we need a student with a talent for acting because this is a play."

Miz Epperson cast Bess as one of the ladies of Bethlehem so she would be in the play, too. Gloria would play Joseph. She would also be in charge of costumes—Gloria *loved* being in charge—and Miz Epperson made her the boss of costuming because Gloria's father would buy or donate whatever his little girl said the school needed. Gloria was thrilled to have her name in big letters in the program.

Roy played a Wise Man. We had to stay after school every day to rehearse. Miz Epperson was smart; by making me the star, and making me learn so much in such a short time, she deprived me of the chance to act out and make a fool of myself. I fell more and more deeply in love with Bess, and began to wonder if girls could marry each other. I knew I wanted to marry Bess and gaze at her blonde loveliness forever. But if we got married, we would have to hire someone to come in and clean our house.

Roy, Bess and I spent endless hours together. Soon I fell about half in love with her. Roy by then had decided he and I were boyfriend and girlfriend; he could tell that I was looking at her much the same way he was looking at me, and he started getting jealous. I liked it that he could tell that I had those feelings for another girl and that he accepted me and my lesbian lust—he was still loved me even though I was in love with another female. Even back then I knew I would always fall in love with other girls.

He liked the fact that, as an actor, he got to pretend that he was someone other than Roy the Sundown country boy. He and I had that much in common.

Our Christmas play was a big deal in Sundown. All the mums came; the thing was so important that they even took time off work to see it. Gloria Spper's father, our biggest benefactor, sat in the best seat, front row center. Reenie and Annie came to admire me in my Virgin Mary getup and Roy in his robes. He and I were so thrilled about being on stage that we almost couldn't keep still. We both giggled in the dressing room as they put makeup, rouge and lipstick on us. Roy knew he wasn't supposed to like wearing makeup, and that was half the fun of it. I reminded him that as a Wise Man he wore a beard, and his beard affirmed his masculinity even if he was wearing lipstick. He nodded that he understand and suggested that when we get old enough we should run away together to the big city and try to become famous actors. That way, we could wear pretty clothes and makeup all the time and never have to pick potatoes again. "We'll be so great in this show," I told him, "that theatre people everywhere will know our names."

Gloria sneered at us. "Dream on, you two. Everyone will notice *me* because of my beautiful costume."

"Nobody will pay you any mind because you're playing Joseph and nobody cares much about him," Roy retorted.

"They'll walk away saying, 'That wonderful actress made me care about Joseph.' Anyway, the Virgin Mary is an overrated part. All she does is sit there and rock Jesus. People will keep forgetting she's there. Any dumdum can play her. It takes real talent to make people care about Joseph, especially when the actor is female."

Just then Miz Epperson hurried up to us. "The curtain is about to go up. Darcie, Sharon, get ready."

As soon as the curtain rose, I heard a hundred hushed female voices. Above them all, Big Mouth

Annie's half-whisper asked, "Isn't she lovely?"

Yes, I was. I gazed down at the Baby Jesus like the most convincing Actors' Studio liar as Gloria, my worst enemy, stood over me, digging her fingernails into my shoulder. Music began playing and the Wise Men walked in with appropriate solemnity. Roy gave me a gift, said something and Gloria repeated it, even though she was supposed to remain silent. Roy did his best not to scratch at the beard that was driving him nuts, and I rocked my baby so hard that the little plastic Jesus infant tumbled onto the floor. Joseph/Sharon started ragging on me about being an unfit mother, so I shot back, "Shut up or you'll wake the baby." Miz Epperson threw her hands up the air and the shepherds exchanged glances. She shoved them out to us, and they spoke their lines. Then one of them got so nervous that he urinated onstage. "You can't do that! Go back to the hills!" yelled Joseph. "He can whiz wherever he wants to," I said. "This a stable, remember?" Sharon tried to force the skid off the stage with her staff, but I grabbed her stick, cast it aside and wrestled with her for a moment or two before getting her by the shoulder and back and flinging her into the audience. I'd kicked her ass once already; shame on her for challenging me again.

Miz Epperson rushed onto the stage and said, "I think it's time for all of us to sing Christmas carols."

Sharon lay prostrate by the folding chairs. I started to sing along with everyone else until Miz Epperson pulled me into the wings. I hoped she wouldn't slap me.

"I know Sharon can be difficult at times, Darcie, but you really shouldn't have thrown her into the audience." Then she walked away. Roy came up to me and said, "You got off easy. Auntie Reenie and Annie are probably waitin' to ream you."

Yes. Reenie practically spat at me, she was so enraged. She kept me inside and made me do all manner of women's work. As I did those chores, I wondered the best way to ask Bess Lindstrom to marry me. I decided to do it the old-fashioned way: Just ask.

On the next Monday, Roy walked Bess and me home from school. Halfway there, I gave him some change and told him to bugger off to the store and buy himself an ice cream bar. He nodded and took off; like other fat kids, he loved goodies.

"Bess," I said, "have you ever thought of getting married?"

She shrugged. "One day." Then, "I'll get married and have a half-dozen kids. I'll wear an apron and slave over a stove. I will marry a handsome man."

"A handsome man, eh? What's his name?"

"I haven't met him yet."

"I have an idea: Why not marry me? I'm not a man, but I'm pretty as can be."

"Oh, I don't girls are allowed to marry other girls."

"Why not?"

"It's against the law or something."

"Laws are made to be broken. Anyway, you're my favorite person and I'm yours. So we should get married."

"We can be each other's favorite person without getting married. We can marry handsome men and still be best friends."

"No." I put my hands on my hips. "We can do whatever we want. We can get married to each other if that's what we want. If other people don't like it, screw 'em. Roy and I are going to run away from home and become famous actors. If we make lots of money. If you're rich, people don't screw around with you. They don't tell you what to do. Do you understand me?"

"Yes."

"Good. Then let's kiss like they do in the movies and we'll be engaged."

We threw ourselves into an awkward embrace and kissed. My heart pounded.

"Did that make you feel weird?" I asked her.

"A bit."

"Let's try it again." We did, and my heart hammered so hard that I swore I'd drop dead right there and then.

Thereafter, we went into the woods after school. Even at that age we knew enough to do our making out in private. Roy got upset because I had stopped walking home with him. One afternoon he followed us into the woods and caught us in action.

"Ha! I see what you're doin'! I'm gonna tell everyone about it!"

"Well, Roy, why would you want to *do* such a thing? Maybe you should try it yourself. You might end up coming out here with us every day."

He looked from me to Bess and back again. Was I putting him on, or had I just made him a legitimate offer? "I'm not interested in kissin' girls."

"Then kiss the boys. Seriously, give us a try. Kissing the girls is lots of fun. You don't know what you're missing."

He thought for a moment. "Do I got to close my eyes?"

"Yes. It's no fun otherwise."

"Which one do I kiss first?"

"That's up to you."

"I'll do you first. I know you better." He leaned over and gave me the worst kiss ever.

"Roy, that sucked. Your lips were all dry and tight."

Bess, laughing, reached out and pulled Roy into her arms. She gave him a long, passionate kiss. I could see him loosen up and lean into it.

"Check this out," said Bess, letting Roy go and pulling me close. We kissed and kissed as if we'd been doing it all our lives. She released me and I kissed Roy again. He did a bit better but still needed lots of experience.

"How does your heart feel?"

"My heart's fine, but my stomach's empty."

"Maybe kissing affects boys differently," said Bess.

From then on, the three of us went into the woods each day to get busy. Alas, Roy failed to become a competent kisser. Bess and I had great sessions, but after a while I felt that kissing wasn't enough, that there should be more, but until I figured out what came next, I just kept on bussing. Bess had other ideas. She instructed me to lie flat on my back while she lay on top of me, then she sealed her mouth over mine and I knew we were on to something good. But then that fat bastard Roy got on top of us and I thought he'd shatter my ribs. I wanted Bess on top me again with her sweet kisses when Roy was elsewhere.

He said, "Let's don't tell anyone that we've been kissin' in the woods, and don't say nothin' about goin' off to become famous actors. They'll just stop us from runnin' away together." The adults *did* keep us from running away together, but it had nothing to do with our making out in the woods.

On one dreadfully cold February night, the grownups called us into the kitchen. Reenie said, "We're moving to Ontario as soon as school is out. We're not gettin' ahead at all here, and we think there would be a better life there. We wouldn't have a farm, so you would become city kids." Then they sent us off to bed. I thought Ontario was as good a place as any to move to; I just didn't want to leave Bess.

The next day I told Bess and she said it was too bad. I agreed but assured her that it was a done deal; nothing I could say or do would alter these plans. We agreed to keep going out the woods until moving day.

When the big day arrived, the roads were muddy and the sky gray. Reenie and Annie spent many hours going through the house, getting rid of this and that, packing things we wouldn't need till we got to Ontario. As our time together ended, I felt less enjoyment of my afternoons in the woods with Bess. It seemed to me that, so far as physical intimacy went, I had started something wonderful but needed to do and learn more before leaving town. I told Bess as much, and she invited me to spend the night at her house. She had her own bedroom, so as soon as her parents went to sleep we would be able to do as much as we wanted.

We said goodnight to her parents and right away began making out. We must have gone at it for hours but I lost all track of time; all I cared about was the feel of her lips on mine.

"Let me get on top," she murmured.

46

"O.K." Then, "What are you doing?"

"Taking off my jammies."

"So I'll be naked. Take off yours, too."

I giggled.

"What's funny?"

"I was just thinking about what your mum and dad would think if they could see us now."

"And what we've been doing in the woods every day after school."

I giggled again. "They wouldn't like it."

"They would kill you. Not me, you. They don't think you're a regular kind of girl anyway. They would blame you for kissing me and touching me."

Presently we were naked and it was so good to feel her naked skin on mine. She dug her tongue into my mouth and all I could do was let out a long deep moan.

"Feels good, eh?"

"Mmmmm."

Then she touched me all over. I knew nothing of masturbation but when she started rubbing and caressing me between my legs, I arched my back and struggled not to scream. I thrashed from side to side, sweating and gasping for air, but Bess just did my thing harder and faster.

The next morning we went to school, two smug Grade 6 girls playing I've Got a Secret. I fell asleep once or twice, and Roy woke me up by jabbing me in the back with his pen. Bess just gazed at me with her blonde loveliness, and I thought: I can't move. I can't leave her. I just can't do it.

But we did exactly that. Bess even came by to say goodbye. I threw my arms around her, kissed her and got into our truck. We wrote to each other a few times and did our best to forget each other. I didn't see her again until many years later.

6

We took our sweet times as we drove across Canada. I would have gone bananas from boredom except that I thought of movies I had seen in which the characters traveled across whichever country they were in. One thing I knew for sure: If you leave home, you're going to meet many people from different places, who believe different things. They're strangers to you and you're a stranger to them, and that's something you have to deal with.

I remember a movie in which a girl not totally unlike myself was in the Deep South during segregation. She went to use the ladies' room and her mum pulled her away, saying, "You have no sense, girl. That one's for colored people only. You stay out of those places."

"This is the Deep South," said the father. "It's different from where we come from. The coloreds and whites are two different classes of people. You do not mix with the colored though you should be polite if you ever have to speak to one. Your mother was just trying to explain to you how things are down here."

"Down here is pretty much the same as up

home," the daughter said. "It's just that up home they didn't have restroom signs saying 'white' or 'colored.'"

"Shut up," said the mother.

"I will not," the daughter said. "I'm just stating a fact: There's the same Jim Crow stuff up north, they just don't admit it. I'm not going to pretend we didn't have Jim Crow up home."

"Well, we won't talk about it any longer," the father said. "Jim Crow will go away when it's ready."

"Just don't talk to niggers," said the mother. "And don't lend them any money, either."

"Live and let live," said the father. "That's all I have to say about it. Live and let live."

I suppose we were excited once we reached Ontario, but not for long. It seemed as boring and depressed as Sundown, and I thought for a moment about that novel I had once read, *The Grapes of Wrath*, about an Okie family that moves out to California because they think they'll be better off, and then they get there and find out they're even worse off.

Gib got a job putting shingles on houses, and the company soon asked him to move to another town not terribly far away. He agreed, so he, Roy and Eddie went there and lived in a trailer that looked like a big dead silver insect. We didn't live in a trailer but we moved into a dilapidated house near the Ontario Power Company and endured its humming until we got so used to it that we managed to tune it out.

Each weekend we drove up to see Gib, Roy and Eddie or they came down to see us. Roy showed me the rifle he'd gotten and he seemed to think he was pretty hot stuff. Eddie now had a job at a gas station, and I mostly just hung out at Dominion Park because there was nothing else for me to do and Reenie refused to buy me a gun.

That September I began classes at Royal High School. Its teachers were old and tired, and I sat there bored shitless. At first I hung back and checked out the crowd before making any friends—"to see who was cool and who was a fool," as Bess would have said. I encountered a surprisingly large number of affluent kids at Royal High. One could recognize them by their quality clothes and proper speech. I had paid enough attention in English class by then to know good grammar from bad. They stayed away from the country kids. I held myself aloof from everyone. I was far from rich but couldn't relate to the poor kids, so that left me by myself. At least then I knew who I was dealing with.

Back in Sundown, I had trouble calling one person better or worse than the others. Well, maybe Sarah Speer had more than the others, but mainly everyone had the same as everyone else. Here, the school's line between haves and have-nots was as visible as big, yellow crime-scene tape. My family had no money, so I couldn't infiltrate the rich kids' cliques. I spent my entire school year trying to figure out how to take care of myself in my new community, but I *did* figure things out.

The main thing I did was make top grades, and that counted for plenty. Nobody got into college without superior grades. Even in Grade 6, the rich kids talked about college, even about applying to the best American schools. If I got the best grades, I could win a scholarship and go to the college of my

51

choice. I also needed to stop speaking the way we did at home, which is to say I had to quit talking like a Sundowner. Well, actually, I had never really talked like a Sundowner—Reenie and Burl, the two most vulgar and gauche people I had ever met, talked like Sundowners, and my insistence on using proper English had rankled Reenie for years. Anyway, I also needed clothes, and when I told Reenie that I didn't want two-dollar blouses from the discount store, she didn't get mad. Maybe she felt glad that I was starting to outgrow my tomboy thing and mature into some sort of lady. "We'll go to one of the uptown stores and get you a few good things." We did just that, and while I did tend to wear the same items fairly frequently, I always wore good stuff. I knew I couldn't go to school and become popular by having kids over to my house because they'd be driven insane by the power station's humming. Anyway, I didn't have much use for those snobs. I concluded that I needed to become the school cutup, the funniest kid around. The best way of gaining people's admiration and liking was to make them laugh. My plan worked; even the teachers responded to my humor.

Towards the end of Grade 8, Roy and I agreed that our plan to run away together and become famous actors probably wouldn't happen. One weekend afternoon, we went down to see him, Gib and Eddie. The flowers were in full bloom and everything was quite colorful. Roy and I went fishing by the canal. He wasn't nearly as fat as before, and he wore his hair longer, almost down to his shoulders.

"So," I asked him, "is it true that you're flunking out?"

He nodded. "My old man is raggin' on me to do better. School's a fuckin' joke. They're not teachin' anythin' worth learnin'. I wanna make a few bucks and buy a motorbike like Gregg's."

"I want one too."

"Girls shouldn't have bikes."

"Kiss my ass, Roy. I'll buy whatever I want and drive it over everyone who says I'm not supposed to own such a vehicle."

Roy turned around and looked at me for several moments. "I think you're a dyke."

"Could be you're right. Well, what of it?"

"Well, you seem like a tomboy even though you shouldn't be one anymore. You're past that age. You should be vain and girlish like all the other chicks."

"Speak to me with respect, fat boy. Remember, I can still take you in two minutes." His face went red, as it always had when I threatened him with a whupping. I added, "How come you're so interested now in my being ladylike and feminine?"

He shrugged. "I'm just tryin' to figure out how men and women are supposed to act. I'm tryin' to act like a man, but you don't exactly act like a woman, so I get confused."

"You act your way and I'll act mine. How's *that* for sound advice?"

"I hear ya. It's just that I'm chickenshit and you're not. You could drive around town in a Hummer and stick your middle finger at everyone who looked at you the wrong way. You just don't give a shit. I'm not like you. I don't want people laughin' at me or pointin' their fingers at me." He burst into tears and I pulled him in close. We sat there for the longest time under the sun by that smelly canal.

"Hey, guy, what's up with those tears? It can't be over whether I'm a dyke or not. What's going on? Talk to me."

"My head's all fucked up. There's the gang at school. They're all tough guys, and if they get the feeling I'm a wimp, I'm dead for sure. Their thing is to smoke, swear and fix cars. I'm O.K. with the cars, but I don't like to swear and smoke. If I don't do those things, they'll say, 'He's a fuckin' faggot!'"

"Do you mean 'fuckin' faggot' as in a gay boy who gives blow jobs?"

He nodded. "There's this one guy who's tall and skinny and weak. He likes school and does good in English. The tough guys are all, like, 'He's such a pansy. Let's work him over after school.' I'm afraid one day they'll say, 'Roy is a fuckin' pansy, too,' and they'll lay into me."

"So you're letting those retarded jocks tell you who to be. That's pretty sad. Let's just wait till we graduate, then we can move to a big city and do our own thing."

"I don't know if I can cope with this shit for that long. See, Darcie, you're different from me. You can go into any situation and become whoever you need to me. You can be successful and make it work out."

"It's been hard for me, too. This move from Sundown to Ontario? I'm not sure what good it's done any of us." Then, "You seem to be bring up this sexual-orientation shit a lot. You called me a dyke, and now you're scared to death that the punks at school will think you're gay. Wanna talk about that?"

"I'm confused because I had an experience at the gas station. There's a customer named Gregg, he's a rough-and-tumble biker guy, all buffed out, farthest thing from a fairy you ever saw. Well, he invites me to go on a ride on his Harley. Anyway, long story short, he gives me this blow job and I like it a lot. So now I'm thinking, 'Am I a flamin' faggot?'" He added, "I'm tellin' you this 'cause you've flown your true colors high and proud. You're a chick that likes chicks. Remember Bess Lindstrom and all those afternoons in the woods?"

"Have you seen Gregg since that blow job?"

"Yeah. I tried to stay away from him because he might come back for more and I might say yes. So he did come by and he tried to kiss me. I backed away, because even though I liked that blow job, I sure as shit am not gonna kiss a man. But he was, like, 'Want another blow job?' and I was, like, 'Yeah, whatever.'"

"Then keep saying yes to those blow jobs but don't tell anyone."

"Yeah, that's probably what I'm gonna do. I'm way too horny all the time."

"Roy, have you made it with a chick yet?"

"Just once. This skanky blonde whore. It wasn't jackshit. Have you been bangin' anyone?"

"No. It's very different for girls. I want to start making it with boys, but they talk so damn much, they would run their mouths and soon Reenie or Annie would find out."

"You don't sound too worried about gettin' knocked up."

"A pregnancy is the easiest thing in the world to prevent."

"Do you think I'm a fag?"

"I think you are you. I think you should aim to be the best Roy you can be, and that should be your life's work. If Gregg has feelings for you, take it as a compliment. If someone dislikes you, just ignore them because they obviously don't know you very well."

"Have you ever been in love?"

"I think I was in love with Bess, but I was a child and that was way back when."

He smirked. "Yeah, you're a dyke. I knew it all along."

"Want me to kick your balls up through the roof of your mouth? I'd be happy to do so."

"You'll never have many friends because you like runnin' your mouth so much and you don't give a shit what you say to people."

"Too bad for me, then."

"I got somethin' to ask you."

"Ask."

"Maybe we could scratch each other's itch," he said.

"Meaning…?"

"Well, you wanna do a guy and I wanna do a chick, so why don't we screw each other?"

"Yuck."

"Why you say that? Don't you like me?"

"Sure I like you. You're my oldest friend. I just don't want to have sex with you."

"Don't matter if you think I'm handsome or ugly. We're best friends an' we'd just be doin' each other a favor."

"Where would we go? How would we avoid getting caught?"

"There's this shack behind the lots? We'll go there. Eddie's the only person who goes there."

"Well, it'll have to do." He led me to the shack, inside of which lay a rotten-looking mattress on the floor. I shrugged and nodded. Roy pulled out his dong and shoved me to the floor.

"Roy, you goof, don't you want to get naked first?"

"Do I have to?"

"Yes. You're not putting it inside me unless I can see what I'm getting."

"You win." He tugged at his apparel until it eventually came off. I pulled off my duds in a few seconds.

He looked me up and down. "Darcie, you're such a pretty girl. You got a face like a movie star. No fat on you at all. Your tummy's tight. Only thing is, you got small titties."

"Titties are overrated."

"I hear that. I think big titties are ugly, anyway."

Naked, he got down on the mattress and snuggled with me. He gave me a big messy kiss that made me think he had learned zero from me and Bess back in the Sundown woods. Well, at least he got a boner. He mounted me and prepared to begin coitus.

"Roy, have you ever heard of something called 'foreplay'? It's where they make out for a while before penetration happens."

"Don't tell me what to do, O.K.? You're a virgin and I'm not, so let me handle this my way." I didn't bother to tell him about my experiences with Bess, so I just said, "Yes, boss." Roy panted and sweated. All those sex books I had read said that a girl's first time was supposed to hurt, but this encounter didn't. In fact, having Roy's schlong inside me felt pretty good, although not as good as Bess's finger rubbing my clitoris. I closed my eyes and felt her soft, moist lips on mine. I missed her *so* much.

Roy finished up and got off me. "Well, that was sure better than that blonde whore I porked."

"I'll take that as a compliment." I felt like adding, "That wasn't jackshit compared to how Bess turned me on." I concluded that I was a dyke, a lesbian, a muff diver. But why, I wondered, did people get so uptight over something that felt so good? I wasn't hurting anyone by being a lesbian, so why was it such an awful thing? Boggles my mind. But I'm not going to make any conclusions about sex based on this one little tryst with Roy. I'll screw him a few dozen more times, then go out there and pick up as many men and women and give each of them a jump. Question: Could I find that many men and women who'd get it on with me? I resolved to find out.

I leaned over to Roy and grabbed his cock. "Let's do it again."

He blanched. "You're not supposed to grab my cock!"

"Why not?"

"Because ladies aren't supposed to grab guys' cocks."

"I'm a dyke, not a lady. I thought we knew that. Now shut up and get a boner."

He did, and he did much better than before. "Don't tell anyone about this," Roy said as we returned to the trailer.

"You're getting good at fucking," I told him. "But we need to do it lots more. We're both such beginners."

Back at the trailer, Annie dished out dinner and asked if we'd been at the canal all day. "How did you do?"

"O.K.," I said. "We did our best, but we need

more practice."

Roy nearly coughed up his milk.

7

Roy kept flunking school, and I busied myself with extracurricular activities that occupied my weekends, so we saw very little of each other. I was O.K. with that because he had started turning into the very sort of redneck of whom he'd been so contemptuous. He seemed to believe that he owned me simply because we continued having sex. Then he bought a motorcycle and became enraged when I learned to ride it better than he did. He said I wasn't nothing more than a dyke and why didn't I just fuck off? Gregg had left town for good, and Roy said he hadn't let a man come near him since, so my friend was very smug and arrogant in his heterosexuality. He had also found a girlfriend at school, so he kept on crowing about her. I called him an asshole and added that his bike needed several hundred dollars' worth of repairs or it would keel over and die while he and his girlfriend cruised around town.

Except for Roy's idiocy, I had a fine life. I belonged to clubs and had friends. My best friend, Caroline Sears, was the school's Miss Nice Girl. She made me ill much of the time, but she loved the cinema as much as I did, so our big thing was watching every movie in town, then picking it apart. I started to think that maybe I had a future as a great filmmaker, but I still clung to my ambition of becoming Canada's first woman prime minister. Caroline was tall and thin, with long brown hair and cobalt-blue eyes. She laughed nonstop at my clever observations and wisecracks, but then everyone found me hilarious. A deeply religious young woman, she, in many ways, was someone I had little use for. A cheerleader, she spent endless hours practicing at something I regarded as beyond trivial.

Penny Conners, one of my other best friends, tall and muscular, like a competitive swimmer, but far too lazy ever to become competent at athletics. She ate all the time and all the wrong kinds of foods. She had dirty blonde hair and lovely hazel eyes, but her best feature was her utter irreverence. She and I seemed made for each other, but I was infatuated with Caroline, and Penny was devoutly hetero. She talked all the time about her interest in men; she talked all the time, period; she reminded me of Big Mouth Annie.

One night, the three of us decided to go ditch our boyfriends. We'd go to the movies and get gooned. Caroline shrugged and said she'd do it, but only because we were women who wouldn't try to have our way with her when she was drunk and vulnerable. Throughout our evening together, I kept thinking about what a pretty girl Caroline was, especially as she stood next to ungainly Penny.

After the picture ended we drove out to some lake and passed around a bottle of Smirnoff's that Penny had pilfered from her father's liquor cabinet.

Caroline took a swig and made a face. "Yuck.

Tastes awful. Why didn't you tell me?"

"It tastes bad because it's poison," said Penny. She took the bottle and said, "My old man drinks this because it has, like, no odor at all. It's water to him."

"Why does he drink so much?" Caroline asked.

"Because when he drinks," Penny said, "he forget how miserable he is."

"And why is he miserable?"

"Because he just is. He and my mother fight like hell all the time. I think they're both screwing other people, and they cheat because they like to know that they're attractive to other people. I guess they think their best years are long gone and that their lives are full of problems that will only get worse. So they drink."

"Penny, that's awful!" said Caroline. "You shouldn't say such things about your parents."

"Well, you asked."

"Fuckin' A," I said, belching.

"Do *your* parents get drunk and fight, Darcie?"

"No, but I wish they would. They'd be more fun."

Penny howled, and Caroline swallowed a big laugh.

"Caroline," I said, "now it's time for you to 'fess up about *your* people."

She took a deep breath. "Well, my mum got remarried last year and they're still in love. You know what? One night I overheard them in their bedroom having sex!"

"Have you ever had sex?" asked Penny.

"No. It's a sin to have premarital sex."

"Says who?" Penny smirked.

"The New Testament."

63

"Therefore it must be true."

"Have you two ever done it?" Caroline asked.

Penny and I shot each other a glance. She said, "I cannot tell a lie. I have done the dirty deed."

Caroline appraised her with wide-eye, can-you-believe-this shit? wonder. "For real?"

"Tell us about it," I said.

"Bram Samuels from school. We drove around looking for a motel where they didn't give a shit if you were married or not. So we get checked in and go to our room, which is tacky as hell, and Bram takes out this mickey of rum and says, 'Let's talk.' I'm nervous as hell because I'm going to get banged for the very first time, and he wants to *talk!* Well, we have our drink and flirt a bit, and he says, 'How about a kiss?' So we start making out and rolling around on the bed, and soon enough he has this boner, so it's time for us to get naked. Bad idea—he tries to rip my clothes off, so I stop him before my buttons go popping all over the place. He asks if I'm protected and I say yes, so he nods and gets himself ready to slip it to me. Well, I have to say that he did O.K., but it wasn't the kind of thing they write songs about. My very first time was a disappointment, to tell the truth."

"Too bad for you," said Caroline. "It's supposed to be the most wonderful, most glorious—"

"Zip it," said Penny.

"My first time," I told them, "didn't hurt at all. but I probably ruptured mine on a horseback or motorbike."

"Who with?" Penny asked.

"I've been riding the same dick since the eighth grade."

"At least you're honest," Penny said. "Tricia Jude has gone down on everyone and yet she acts like Little Miss Innocent. She makes me want to barf." She looked at the empty bottle of vodka and said, "This soldier is dead. Anyone got any ideas on how to get another one?"

"We could steal some if we looked around and found an unsuspecting couple," I said.

"Too dangerous," Penny said. "Let's go back."

Caroline got up, the nearly fell back down. The poor chick couldn't hold her booze. She threw herself on me and I held her up. She grabbed my breast and I wondered if she was sweet on me or something.

"So," Penny asked, "who's gonna drive back?"

"Well, Caroline's too gooned, so I guess that leaves me," I said.

Penny nodded. "Then I'll fall asleep and dream of sexy men."

We all got in, and Caroline fell asleep in the back seat. "As long as she doesn't barf, we'll be O.K.," said Penny. "I hate it when people vomit. I take it as a sign of weakness."

As we got closer to town, I stopped at a red light and said, "Penny, doesn't that car look like Mr. Glover's?"

She nodded. "That's his ride, and that's him. But that's not Mrs. Glover; that's Mrs. Eldridge, and he's got his arm around her."

"You're right! It is!" I honked the horn and waved at them.

"What the *fuck*, Rota? You wanna get us kicked out of school?"

"Just watch what I'm doing."

"You're fuckin' gooned; that's your problem."

"No. I'm immune to the effects of alcohol."

He and she looked our way, then looked away. When the light turned green, he sped off.

"We are *fucked* come Monday." Said Penny. "Why did you do that, Rota? Have you been eating retard sandwiches again?"

"We don't have to worry; they do," I explained. "We caught them cheating on their spouses. Shame on them."

Penny frowned. "Maybe so. In that case, good on us. You think we should tell Caroline about this?"

"No, it's best just to let her keep respecting Glover.

"Yeah. In fact, we won't tell anyone at all."

When we got Caroline home, we had to carry inside because she was too fucked up to walk. Penny drove me home, and the next morning we met over a cup of coffee to promise each other to shut up about what we had seen the night before. But then, in the middle of homeroom, there comes this message over the public-address system: "Will Darcie Rota and Penny Conners please come to the principal's office after homeroom."

We looked at each other for a few moments, then shrugged and got to our feet. When we got to the office, Penny had to see Mrs. Cleaver while I saw Mr. Glover. Mrs. Cleaver, in her mid-forties, was a pretty woman who reminded me of Jane Fonda. I could understand why our principal was horny for her. I wanted to give her a jump myself. She greeted me with a big nervous smile and asked me to sit down.

"Darcie," she said, "you are one of our most distinguished athletes. You're an A student and you've proven yourself to be a very capable leader. Next year you will be eligible more many scholarships and I hope you get them because, frankly, I know that your family is financially pinched."

"Yes, ma'am."

"I want to help you, Darcie. I want to write your college-recommendation letters and help you apply for the scholarships of your choice. A 'full ride' scholarship is what I have in mind."

I nodded. "I would be grateful for your help."

"Have you decided yet what you want to study?"

"I'm torn between filmmaking and law. The problem is, with filmmaking, the best schools are in New York and California."

"Well, you need to start thinking it over. I believe that the best colleges are in America and they are always eager to accept Canadian students because it looks good for them to have foreign students, especially those who have distinguished themselves as much as you have." She added, "Have you thought about running for student-body president next year?"

"President? I thought that was for boys."

She offered me a little smile. "It doesn't have to be."

"I understand Vaughan Garrett wants that job. He's rich and, if necessary, he'll buy himself the election."

"We can deal with that. We can limit the campaign spending."

"Mrs. Cleaver," I said, "don't worry about what I saw the other night. I won't tell anyone."

"Thank you for that."

Our meeting ended, and I stood in the main foyer waiting for Penny. She joined me soon, her walk bouncy and smile smug. "Guess who just became our school paper's new editor?"

"Guess who's going to be next year's student-body president?"

She laughed. "So we both made out all right this morning."

I shrugged. "Not bad for a morning's work."

8

During the summer between Grades 11 and 12, I worked. Penny and Caroline had left town, and Roy, who had finally passed Grade 9, rode down to see me a few times but we didn't have intercourse. I had lost all interest in him; maybe I had simply outgrown him. Often I felt sorry for him—he simply followed the herd, vaguely aware that he was unhappy but clueless about how to improve his life. He loved it that I had been elected student-body president by a ridiculous margin. But our conversations soon lost their momentum and we'd revert to the same tired old subjects—cars, motorcycles, Sundown. "You're the only person I can talk to," he told me. "Even though I've had my cock in your pussy a zillion times, I still think of you as a regular girl. The other chicks I date, it's a night of eating, drinking and screwing. We have nothing else in common. What happens to us after we get married?"

"You talk about the fact that you have nothing to talk about."

"That sounds pretty boring."

"I imagine marriage *is* boring."

I concluded that all he and I had in common

were Sundown and sex. Sometimes I marveled at my own weirdness; Reenie had said, 'You're not my kid; you're a bastard we adopted. You have no kin, no family, no relatives.' Knowing that Roy was not my cousin—and I'm pretty sure I would have screwed him even if he was—I had intercourse with him because I was horny and he was there. I had always known I was deeply attracted to other females, so I hooked up with Bess. All the while I looked in the mirror and said, 'Darcie, you're different from the rest.' I knew that other girls wanted houses, husbands and children. Well, I didn't. I wanted to go through life being Darcie Rota and, if possible, love and be loved along the way. I certainly didn't want to be with any man or woman who pointed at my vagina and said, "That belongs to me."

Reenie and Annie didn't like it at all that I had been elected student president. "I wanted you to be prom queen, and I know you can't be both," she said. Annie said that government was a nasty, corrupt affair that we should leave to the men. I stayed away from our house as much as I could, which was nothing unusual. At home, I had to listen to constant bickering; one night, I came in with a new haircut and Reenie ragged on me for an hour about it. I half-ran out of the house and headed to the car. Reenie threw open the front door and screamed, "Jus' you git away from that car! It don't belong to you! It's your father's!" Burl came outside and said to me, "You wanna go somewheres? I'll take you there."

"Anywhere but here," I muttered as we got into the car. "I'm sick of this place and these people."

We drove out to Lake Huron, got out and sat on a bench facing the Great Lake.

"This is nice," he said, "but I would rather live out by the ocean. It calms me, starin' at the water. The ocean is an amazing thing."

"Whatever," I muttered.

"I got so sick of Sundown. I had to get out. I'm glad I did."

"I guess Ontario is an improvement, but I don't like it here much either."

"You're too restless. You got to get away from us."

"I don't have a chance at being happy here. I want to go somewhere I have a chance at being myself and doing my own thing."

"You and your mum have always clashed and always will. She and I don't clash because I agree with everything she says. That's the way to get along with her."

I shook my head. "I can't do that. I've tried but it doesn't work. Do you know what she was bitching about this time? My new haircut! Is it any of her fucking business if I get a new haircut?"

He shrugged. "All I can say is, you should be a coward like me and go along to get along. You're too much of a fighter and that is going to make your life very difficult. It's Darcie against the world."

"It's always been that way. I'm just someone you took in. I belong to a family of three: Me, myself and I."

"I've tried to be here for you."

"You've rarely been here for me."

"I'm sorry you feel that way."

"I'm sorry, too."

Just then he smiled. "Darcie, I'm very proud of you for what you been doin' at school. You're just doin' the best you can, and that's why your mum thinks you're showin' off. I think you're gonna go into this world and give it hell. Have you figured out where you're gonna go to school next?"

"The principal thinks I can get into an American college. I'm going to wait and see which school makes me the best offer. What am I going to study? Filmmaking or law. Those are the two things that interest me."

He nodded. "Lawyerin' sounds like you. You can out-talk and out-argue everyone, and you always have to be right. Plus, there will always be a need for lawyers in this world. But the filmmaking thing? You got to do that in Hollywood, doncha? That place is bad news, from what I've heard."

"Well, the only way for me or anyone else to get started as a movie director is to go to film school, so being admitted is job one. If I get in and get the filmmaking skills I'll need, I'm sure the instructors will give me guidance about what to do next. As for law, well, I'm sure I could be successful in *that*. It's just that I would much rather make movies I care about than spend the rest of my life practicing law."

"Sounds like you've already made your decision."

"Sounds like."

"What about gettin' married?"

"What about it?"

"You gonna do t?"

"Nope."

He chuckled. "I was expectin' that answer. I couldn't see you playin' wifey, anyway. I also would hate the idea of seein' you with some husband who said, 'Hey, bitch, fix me a turkey pot pie,' and you sayin', 'Yes, dear.'"

"Never gonna happen. Anyway, if I want to be with a man, I'll go out and get one for the night."

"Well, my advice is, ride as many dicks as you want but don't go talkin' about it afterwards. Plus, don't say a word about it around Big Mouth Annie, 'cause she'll spread it all over town." He went quiet for a moment and cleared his throat. "Darcie, I'm goin' on sixty years old now, so my life is damned near over and I have very little to show for it. I get low when I think about it. I can remember when I was sixteen, and it seems like yesterday. To you I must seem ancient but I can't believe I'm this old. You should go out into this world and do as you please regardless of what others say. I've worked my whole life and have somethin' close to nothin' to show for it. Go out there an' give 'em hell, kid. If they don't like what you say or do, tell 'em to kiss your ass."

I leaned over and kissed his stubbly cheek. "Your problem," I told him, "is that you keep listening to all those bullshit Gipper things."

July was a hot month for us. My life went mostly according to my wishes, and Burl went to work. He told everyone that his daughter would become the premier of Ontario or even prime minister of Canada one day.

One night I went to bed just before midnight and felt myself shaken awake, then slapped across the face. Droplets of water hit my face. "Darcie! Get up! Your father's dead!" I heard Reenie say in a freakish hoarse scream. Annie got behind her and managed to pull Reenie off me. Annie said, "You better go out there now if you want to see him 'cause the ambulance guys are takin' him away." I hurried into my skimpy bathrobe and rushed into the living room. There he lay, my father's face blue.

"Why is he that color?"

"Heart attack. Happened all of a sudden," said the paramedic. "He lived just long enough to wake Reenie."

He checked me out and licked his lips at the sight of my mostly uncovered thighs. It didn't matter to him that my father had just died; to this guy, I was just another piece of sixteen-year-old pussy. They left us with plenty of sedatives for Reenie, but she just kept waking up and crying out, "Where is he? Where is my Burl?" Annie and I couldn't sleep, so we sat up and made funeral arrangements. She kept looking at me as if expecting me to burst into tears at any moment; if I had done so, she would have said, "Come now, Darcie, you've got to pull yourself together and be strong for your mum." But since I showed no emotion except sleepiness, she surely wanted to say, "You're a cold one, aren't you? You didn't care about Burl because he wasn't your birth father. You were adopted, and adopted children have no feelings for their adoptive parents." I could have retorted, "How does it feel to be known as Big Mouth Annie, the woman who is so tactless and indiscreet that she simply repeats everything she overhears? You've been a laughingstock for as long as I've known you, so I don't think you have any right to criticize anyone else, least of all *me*."

We had the funeral on a Sunday. Burl looked handsome in his spiffy clothes and we rode in a big white Continental. Reenie, grinning in spite of herself, said, "Seems like someone has to die before we get dressed up and ride in a fancy car." I added, "Too bad he couldn't be alive to see this. All those people crying over him, giving him the V.I.P. treatment." Reenie laughed; Annie shook her head at me. For all our fights, Reenie and I could laugh together sometimes, too.

Loneliness and despair settled over our house like a pall of toxic smoke right after Burl's death. Reenie burst into tears a dozen times each day right up until I went back to school. I tried hanging out for a while just to keep her company, but she turned on me, as if I had somehow caused her husband's death. She laid into me about remaining dry-eyed at the funeral, about continuing with my serious ambitions in life and my refusal to settle for an office job and mundane lifestyle. I got fed up and stayed out for hours at a time; she ragged on me for failing to be there for her.

Two weeks into school, I sat at home reading a Saul Bellow novel and kept checking the clock because they were expecting me at an afternoon meeting and I needed to head back to school soon. I kept reading the book, expecting Burl to get home, and then I reminded myself that we'd buried him and he wouldn't come home again, ever. I started to miss him, and wiped the tears off my face before they stained my book.

Just then I heard our car pull up and its doors open and close. The two women kept grousing at each other about how expensive everything was. They came in and saw me sitting there with my book in my lap.

"Why you look all down and out?" Reenie asked.

"Book made me sad."

"You read too much," she said. "Always got your

nose in one of those things. Been that way all your life. Too much reading makes your brain go funny. You know that?"

I nodded. "I hear ya, Mum."

She held up some fake flowers. "Got these at the discount store. They're cheaper than the real ones and last forever. They're for Burl's grave."

"Very nice. I need to go back to school." I hurried out the door, and heard Annie say to Reenie, "That girl's a weird one. Don't shed a tear over her father's death but she cries when she's readin' a sad story."

9

Grade 12, my senior year, was just too easy and too much fun. Penny and I went only to those classes we liked; Mr. Glover gave us permission not to attend the ones we didn't like. We went to Advanced English because we liked the teacher, and Caroline went, too. The three of us sat in the front row and competed for the best grades.

Caroline, the school's head cheerleader, often attended class in her uniform. Penny and I nearly laughed at her but had to admit that her status as boss cheerleader made her the most respected girl at the entire school. The three of us dated three boys who were the best of friends. Whenever we three were with them, we clung to their arms and made eyes at them, but in truth we were indifferent to them. We spent so much time hanging out with those boys because we were expected to do so. Caroline grew very uptight because Harry kept pressuring her to have intercourse with him. Penny and I told her to give it up to him, mainly because we were getting tired of listening to her bitch about how he was always trying to feel her up. Penny and I were banging away with our guys and it didn't seem like such a big deal to us. Nobody was supposed to know about what who was doing what with whom in private, but of course everyone did find out soon enough, mainly because the boys loved to brag about it. These boys and their swaggering heterosexuality made me laugh.

Caroline decided, with her unique logic, that if our team won its game against Osoyoos, she would give her cherry to Harry. Well, we did win—destroyed them, in fact—but Caroline, as head cheerleader, walked off the field at the end of it all not with the bright-red face of a girl who'd just been screaming like a maniac. No sirree; her mug looked ashen. Penny and I said, "Be happy! We won!" Then we went to meet our dates, who apparently had checked out the Princeton University Style Manual because they wore short haircuts, Weejuns and loafers. My boyfriend, Blake, wanted pity because he'd gotten a cut on his cheek during the game. I said, "No pity—you should be proud of your battle scar and the three touchdowns you scored." Penny's boyfriend Sam shambled out, and she said, "Here comes my hero!" Harry nearly tripped over his own feet in his rush to see Caroline. She didn't get a chance to congratulate him because he picked her up and gave the longest, hottest, juiciest kiss she'd ever received. Then he loaded her into his car and she gave us a nervous little wave as they sped off. We climbed into Sam's car and headed off for lots of talk over banana splits.

The next morning, my telephone rang at just before nine o'clock. "I need to talk to you immediately," Caroline said.

"Well," I replied, "if you absolutely, positively *need* it, why can't we do it right now?"

"I'm coming over right now. We can talk over breakfast. O.K.?"

"Whatever you say, boss."

Twenty minutes or so later, she arrived looking, well, not so great. "So," I asked, "how is Royal High's newest slut?"

She rolled her eyes. "I guess I survived, but I need to ask you some questions about it."

We went to a pancake house and were served lukewarm eggs and sausage. In a quiet voice, she asked, "Is it always so messy? I mean, I had sticky stuff running down my legs. Harry said, 'Don't sweat it; it's just come.' Was he right?"

I nodded. "Sex is a messy business. Especially the first time. You might say, 'That was so disgusting that I nearly barfed.' But you know something? You go back for more, and more, and more."

"He seemed to do all the work and have all the fun. I just lay there. It seemed very disappointing."

"It can be very disappointing, especially if the person you're with doesn't really know what the hell he's doing. For the next few decades, you will want sex as often as you can get it. As you get more experience, you will figure it out and get more pleasure from it." I added, "You're taking this stuff much too seriously."

She raised her chin. "Sex is a very serious business."

"Sex is a big fucking joke. Unless, of course, you get preggers, and then you have to decide to abort the little bugger or let him live."

"Maybe you're right. Say, you want to go out drinking this weekend?"

"O.K. Will Penny be joining us?" I asked.

"No, she's already committed to doing something else."

"Just the two of us? Yeah, let's do it."

On Friday night we went to the children's playground at Western Park. No one went there late at night, and the cops were too busy hassling the gays—or taking naps—to bother patrolling the playground. I didn't especially like drinking so I took only a few sips, but Caroline got really fucked up. She went from the swings to the monkey cars and did a little striptease. Presently she got down to her pretty pink panties and climbed into the grounded blue jet. She giggled as she pretended to fly the aircraft. I crawled in with her, unable to help noticing what a cute bod she had and how good she smelled.

"Are we having fun yet?" I asked her.

"Too much fun." She swallowed a bug alcoholic laugh. "Say, Darcie, how does Blake kiss you?"

"He kisses me on the lips, of course."

"Want to see how Harry kisses?"

"Well, I—"

She twisted around and gave me the longest, hottest kiss I'd had since Bess Lindstrom in Sundown slapped all those lip-locks on me.

"I doubt he kisses you that way," I said.

"Want another one?" She kissed me again.

"Caroline, what are you doing?"

"I'm teaching you to be a good kisser."

"I'm already pretty good at that." I wanted to add, "We better stop or I'm going to slip my hand into your pretty pink panties and masturbate you till you scream, just like Bess did to me. Is that what you

80

want, Caroline? Maybe it is. Maybe you're a repressed lesbian who's attracted to me, an unrepressed lesbian."

"Nobody is ever good enough at kissing." She bussed me some more, and we really started going at it. Soon we were both naked, and I reached down between her legs, found her clitoris and went to town. She moaned into my mouth as her hands explored my breasts. We loved each other up until the sky lightened. I gathered our clothes and said, "Let's get out of here."

"No. I want to spend a decade fondling your beautiful little titties."

"Are you hungry?"

"All I want to eat is your pussy."

"Well," I told her, "it's breakfast time and *I'm* hungry, so let's get some ham and eggs."

We went to a diner and ordered deluxe breakfasts. As we devoured our food, she said, "You won't tell anyone about last night, will you?"

"Hell no."

"I'd hate to have anyone think we were lesbians."

"Uh, I think we *are* lesbians."

She scowled. "No, lesbians are women who look like men. They're ugly and scary. We're just girls in love."

"Was that your first time with a girl?"

I shook my head. "No, I had a girlfriend back in Sundown. How about you?"

"I met a girl named Kris at summer camp a few months back. She made the first move. I might've resisted and said, 'Get away from me! I'm no dyke!' but she was just so nice to me and I was very horny."

81

"I wonder where she is now."

"Oh, we stay in touch. We want to go to the same college." She eyeballed me. "Darcie, do you think it's possible to love two people at one time. I love you and her."

I shrugged. "I'm not jealous."

"Good. I thought maybe you would be. I thought that when I was masturbating you in that playground it could be considered cheating on Kris."

"Maybe Kris has been masturbating other women in your absence."

"Probably. Know something else? Being with you is much better than being with Harry. *Much* better."

"Damn straight." We laughed and ordered chocolate sundaes at six in the morning.

She began making a point of waylaying me in the school cafeteria and paying excessive attention to me. She seemed to forget that Harry and Penny were there. Harry didn't mind as long as he stuck his cock inside her each weekend. Penny cared a great deal; consequently, I paid more attention to her, which alienated Caroline.

"Are you making it with Caroline?" Penny asked me.

Caroline overheard her. "Excuse me?"

"No," I said, "I am not 'making it' with Caroline, although I do love her and we're the best of friends. If you don't like that, too bad."

"Darcie," Penny asked, "why would she think you and I were fucking?"

I sighed. "Penny, I'll admit it: Caroline and I have been making it." To Caroline I said, "Don't get bent out of shape. You've got Kris."

Penny frowned. "You've been making it with

Caroline? Is that what you said? Did I hear you right?"

I nodded. "You heard right. I make it with Caroline; she makes it with me. I make it with Blake and she makes it with Harry. One of these nights we may even have a four-way."

"Am I the last to know about this?"

I shook my head. "It's a secret. If the world knew about it, they might say—"

"That you're dykes, which apparently you are."

"Penny!" Caroline put her hands on her hips, to show her indignation. "Don't call me a dyke! I'm pretty and feminine and the envy of every girl around. Maybe Darcie is a dyke because she's tall and strong and can probably beat the bejesus of most of the guys we know if it ever came down to a fight. But that's her, not me."

Penny scratched her head. "What do Darcie's height and strength have to do with anything?"

"Well, lesbians are very masculine females. Darcie's one of the prettiest girls around, but she's tall and strong and aggressive and she never acts like a girl. I bet everyone who knows her has already assumed she's a lesbian, so no one would be surprised if she confirmed it. I love Darcie but I am not Darcie. I am not a lesbian."

Penny said to Caroline, "Well, I'm just about twenty pounds overweight, and in every other way I'm as far from being feminine as you can get. So you probably think I'm a dyke, too. Why don't you just come out and say it?"

Caroline threw up her hands. "I was talking about Darcie, not you. You're fat because you eat too much shit and rarely get off your lazy ass. You could lose that flab if you tried hard enough."

"Fuck you, Caroline!" I walked away.

"Darcie, don't go!" Caroline yelled.

Penny caught up with me. "Where are you going?"

"I'm trying to get away from her."

"I've got the family car, so let's go to the park."

I nodded and we drove out to Western Park and sat in the cockpit of the blue jet. I said nothing about my night in there with Caroline. As much as I disliked her sometimes, I had to admit that she was a really great fuck.

"So," Penny asked, "are you O.K. with being a dyke?"

I rolled my eyes. "Do I have to be anything?"

She shook her head. "Guess not. It freaked me out when I figured out you were a lesbian, and I've always prided myself on being more open-minded and enlightened than everyone else. But now that I know about you, I'm not sure if I want to keep being friends with you. I'm wondering if you're going to try to rape me or something."

"Don't worry. You're the last chick in the world I would jump on."

"Good to know—I think." She climbed out of the cockpit. "Come on, I'll drive you home."

"No, I'd rather walk."

"Whatever."

That evening, Caroline called me and had a cry so passionate that she shook me up in spite of myself. Then she apologized a dozen times until I told her to shut the fuck up.

We, the three most popular girls at school, had broken up with our superstar boyfriends, and everyone we knew seemed delightfully scandalized. We wouldn't talk about it, so the gossipmongers were free to invent rumors. One of the busybodies said that Caroline wanted to have a *ménage a trois* with Blake and me but I turned her down. I tried to laugh it off, but I felt sad that so many people believed that bullshit.

As student-body president, I started to wish that I had lost the election. I had a dozen boring bureaucratic chores to do at any time. I longed at times to return to the Sundown potato patch and fuck around with those country kids who were too ignorant to judge you by the clothes you wore or the car you drove. But that Sundown didn't exist for me any longer, except in my head; and anyway, I was scarcely the same Darcie Rota who'd spent all those years there. I had no Sundown to go back to; so where did I belong? In college, though it would probably be even worse than high school, with its rich kids who treat scholarship students like second-class citizens. But I need to go there and get that sheepskin; without it, I'll just be another office flunkie somewhere in southwestern Ontario. Well, fuck that; I need to get a degree and head for a big city. Got to tough it out. That's what Burl used to say—*Tough it out*. It would be so nice to talk to him right now. It would so nice to talk to someone who talked sense instead of talking shit.

When graduation day finally arrived, I received my diploma, and a hug, from Mr. Glover, who went on about the fine work I'd done as student-body president and athlete. He finished his remarks with,

"Before you stands our premier in twenty years." Everyone applauded, and I laughed, because Burl had said the same thing.

10

Gainesville, Florida, was where I ended up after submitting my scholarship documents and whatnot. They offered me a full scholarship plus room and board. Duke, Vassar and Smith also wanted me but not enough to give me a full ride, and since I had no money, I said yes to Gainesville. Reenie and Annie escorted me to the Greyhound bus in Ontario, and a dozen hours later I got off in Florida and walked to my dorm with my one suitcase.

They had placed in me Broward Hall, which was old and ugly, but since it was free I accepted it with gratitude. Right away I met my roomie, a pre-med student named Fiona Packer. Since I had written pre-law on my application, the housing office probably thought we would be a good match. We were, but for all the wrong reasons. We discovered right away that we loved to break the rules, so we did just that, sneaking into and out of our building at the oddest hours. She and I joined sororities and Fiona acted as my campaign manager when I ran, successfully, for student office. We ditched our building and drove for hours in the Mercedes her father had bought her. We drank vodka and talked about the future. "I don't really want to become a doctor," she said. "I just don't want to study humanities like all those idiot girls." Her father also sent her fat checks and she spent plenty on me, mainly because she'd always had far more of everything than she needed and therefore knew little of the value of money. Still, I felt grateful for her largesse. She said, "Darcie, you're a good-looking girl—pretty fuckin' face, great tits, nice ass—but you dress like a bag lady." So she took me to the best ladies' store in town and bought me a new wardrobe.

I didn't realize that Fiona was, or would soon become, an adolescent alcoholic until October. When I asked her why she drank so much, she retorted, "What's it to you?" so I dropped the matter. Her grades declined and she cut classes more often. Fortunately, I'd already done most of the assigned reading, so my good grades were virtually guaranteed. Fiona had no use for studying, and no use for those who did study, so she would run up and down the hallways, screaming, "Study on, you ass-kissing, money-hungry bitches!" Then she'd hurry back into her room, open a bottle of vodka and get even more pissed.

Her sorority started worrying about her when she showed up drunk for a dinner to honor the school's president. She staggered up to him and said, "Hey, dude, wassup? How's it hangin'?" Her parents insisted that she have a weekly heart-to-heart talk with Dani, her older sister. Fiona hated it, resented Dani's condescending manner. One afternoon she came back and slammed the door.

"Rota," she told me, "I just completely fucked up. I had this meeting with fuckin' Dani and told her I'm knocked up. I swore her to secrecy but I'm sure she'll tell our fuckin' parents. They will be *so* pissed!"

"Abortion," I said.

"Yeah, tomorrow I'm going to see the safecracker. I'll need you to drive me. I don't want to go through this thing alone."

I did as told, and by the time we got back to Broward Hall, she said, "I'm feeling weak. You'll have to carry me." So I did, and she said, "You're stronger than I thought."

I cut classes so I could stay near her in case she needed my help. She recovered very fast and said, "I want to go to Jacksonville to get drunk and make trouble. Let's do it."

"Don't be stupid, Fiona. You need to take it easy for the next while."

"Come with me and we'll have a wild time. We'll stay at my house and be back here by Sunday evening."

I nodded. "Just promise me you won't pick up some handsome crazy guy who will rape and murder us."

"No promises."

We started our evening at some funky joint near the U., where a seven-foot black guy asked me to dance and I got cramps all over by looking up at him. Then we went to Molly's, a place named by and for its owner, who nodded at our fake IDs and told us to seat ourselves. We did so, and I noticed right away that the dance floor was packed with same-sex couples.

"Fiona," I said, "this is a gay bar."

"Oh my God!" she replied with mock outrage.

"How did you find out about this place?"

She shrugged. "I discovered it in my travels."

"Are you a lesbian?"

"Negative. I like gay bars because they're more fun than straight ones. Thought I'd show you this one because you're a hick from Canada who probably doesn't get to see such sights."

On the dance floor, we couldn't get into any sort of rhythm because she was too convulsed in laughter. Presently she collected herself and we shuffled around together, but then she started stepping on my feet. "Fuck this shit," I said. "Let's sit down and finish our drinks."

As we neared our table, we found two women standing in front of us. "Don't y'all attend Gainesville? You live at Broward?" one of them asked.

Fiona said that, yes, we did. The women invited us back to their table, and we said yes, but first we needed to go back to our table and fetch the drinks we'd already paid for.

They introduced themselves at Uli and Dot. "Darcie," Fiona whispered, "if Dot tries to pick me up, you be sure to tell her you're my lover. Got it?"

"I hear ya."

Uli and Dot were members of some sorority and came here to get away from everyone they knew. Dot sat there mentally undressing Fiona, who was worth the effort, with her light-brown hair, hazel eyes and deep dimples. Dot had no way of knowing that Fiona's family was rich, or that Fiona was a lush. I didn't know much about this bar scene—I didn't know if I was supposed to offer them drinks or dances or ask them personal questions (in other words, invite them to lie about themselves). Dot said she and Uli had been dating for close to a year.

"How nice for you!" Fiona exclaimed. I nearly

spat out my drink. Fiona, loather of romance and romantics, really made me laugh sometimes. Dot and Uli, taking her seriously, beamed at us and each other.

"You two met in college, right?" Uli asked. "Were you gay before then?"

"I was but Fiona wasn't," I said.

The women told us about which professors were loathsome and which women on campus were closet dykes. At some point Fiona made an excuse for us and we parted company with our new friends. Back at her house, as we lay in twin beds, she asked, "Have you ever done it with a woman?"

"Didn't you hear what I said back there? I've been a dyke for quite some time."

"But you didn't tell me."

"Well, you didn't ask."

Then, "Darcie?"

"Yes?"

"Wanna fuck?"

"Excuse me?"

"You heard me."

"No, Fiona, I don't 'wanna fuck' you."

"Why not?"

"Because I don't fuck straight girls."

"Well, if I want to fuck you, it means I'm not straight." She got up, threw off the covers and said, "If you don't come to me, I'll go to you." She did just that. "Now, what do I do?"

"You mean you don't know?"

"Well, I know this much." She put a long hot kiss on my lips and reached down below, massaging my clitoris.

"You know a lot," I said, and we kissed some more.

We spent the rest of that semester mostly in bed. We got up just to eat and attend class. Fiona studied and improved her grades, because that was the only way we could stay together. She also quit drinking because she realized that drinking was a way for her *not* to feel, and during her time with me she wanted to feel as much and as deeply as she could. Our sororities wondered where were and what we were doing; we were barely legal, deeply in love and oblivious to the rest of the world—but that world knew damn well that *we* existed.

By February, I started to notice that people on our floor had stopped speaking to us. Conversations, in fact, stopped the moment we came into view. Finally, Fiona confronted one of the women and asked, "How come you people don't speak to us anymore?"

"Because you and Darcie Rota spend all of your time in your room."

"Well, what of it?"

"You never come out."

"Well, what of it?" Fiona repeated.

"It's like you're perverts who are horny for each other."

"Well, we are. Is there something wrong with that?"

The girl scowled. "We think it's absolutely disgusting what you two do behind closed doors."

Fiona took a step towards her and the girl ran off, crying. Fiona cackled, shaking her head.

"See what you've done now, Fiona," I said. "She's going to the resident counselor about this. We may get kicked out of school."

"Yeah? Good! This college is a fuckin' joke anyway. We're better off without it."

"Not me. Do you remember me? I'm Darcie Rota, a hick from small-town Canada. This is my only shot at a better life. I gotta graduate and get that fuckin' degree."

"You can do just fine without a degree."

"Like hell I can."

"Here's the deal," she said. "We can go to a private school together. My old man will continue sending checks, and we can both find part-time jobs to keep food on the table. Fuck, I wish he'd double my monthly checks, but that won't happen. I don't give a fuck about my education. Best thing we can hope for is that we make do on his checks plus whatever you and I can make on the side."

"I think you're wrong, but I hope you're right," I told her.

Presently Fiona and I received summonses to appear before people who had the power to harm us. Fiona had to see the resident counselor and I needed to visit Miz Duggan, the dean of students.

"Miz Rota—may I call you Darcie?—I suppose you know why you've been called to my office. There has been an, um, incident in your dormitory. Would you care to explain it to me?"

"Not especially."

"Darcie, this is a very important matter, and your cooperation is essential. My understanding is that you are one of our top students in every way—an achiever. So I'm assuming that you will want to work out this matter immediately and continue with your collegiate career." She added, "I know you're here on scholarship, a very humble Canadian who simply hasn't had the advantages the other girls have enjoyed. Tell me, have you thought of a way to relate better to your roommate?"

"Fiona? We get along just fine. I'm in love with her and she's in love with me."

Her face darkened. "Are you saying that your relationship with Fiona Packer is romantic?"

"It's sexual. We eat each other's pussy."

Her face darkened some more. "I don't appreciate being spoken to that way."

"Well, you asked."

"Lesbianism is something one can overcome."

"Assuming, of course, that one wishes to overcome it."

"Here's what I'm going to do for you," she said. "I'm going to refer you to a psychiatrist here and I'll see you on a regular basis. I want you to know I'm your friend and I'll be cheering for you as you work through your issues.. By the way, have you thought of becoming a mother one day?"

"Why ask me that, especially considering you've never even been married?"

She glowered at me. "This conversation is about you, not me. Anyway, I had many chances, but I chose career over family."

"Well, you're not exactly single. I know you've been shacking up with Miz Maloney in the psych department for the past couple of decades. At least I'm up front about who I am and what I'm after."

Her face was now contorted in rage. "How *dare* you speak to me that way! Just for that, I'm sending you for a psychiatric evaluation right now! You are clearly a pathological personality immediately in need of professional help. Such an attitude you have, especially when I'm trying to help you. You're sicker than I thought."

The campus cops came by and escorted me to the U.'s hospital. They stripped me naked, gave me a gown and locked me in a room with a hole for a toilet and a fluorescent light dangling overhead. Some hours later, Dr. Nasrallah, an Arab psychiatrist, came in to see me. He asked me if I felt suicidal. I said no, but I wanted to get out of there. He nodded and promised that he would let me out as soon as possible. I did some pretending that would have made any Actors' Studio professor proud. I made like I was delighted to see the good doctor and his swarthy, pockmarked face. I told him the most amazing bullshit stories about my hardscrabble life in the Great White North. A few days later, he signed my discharge order and I walked back to Broward Hall.

In my mailbox I found two letters. The first, from my sorority, said, in effect, 'Goodbye. Good luck.' The second letter was from Fiona. I clutched it as I hurried up the stairs to our room. All of her property was gone. I sat on her bed and read her letter.

To My Darling Baby Girl,

The powers that be know about us and, therefore, called Mommy and Daddy and told them. He came to get me and wants me to get some professional help. To him, lesbianism is right up there with schizophrenia and manic-depression as 'mental illnesses.'

Please be free and be yourself, always. I'll remember you forever and know you'll do the same for me.

The following day I received a letter from the scholarship committee informing me that they had terminated my scholarship. They said they assumed I knew why.

I packed my suitcase and left the campus forever. I traipsed down to the Greyhound station by exactly the same route I had taken upon my arrival.

11

My mother was sitting in her recliner when I entered her home. "Don't come in. You're not welcome here. I got this call from some high-up woman down there in Florida and she told me what you were doin' down there. So you jus' turn your queer ass aroun' and go away."

"Mum," I retorted, "all you know is what they told you. Don't you want to hear *my* version?"

"That woman said you were eatin' pussy down there. Why would she lie about such a thing?"

"Mum—"

"You have nothin' to say that I'd care to hear. Why did you come back here, anyway? I don't want you in my life. You're a disgrace."

"You're the only family I have. Where else could I go?"

"Go back to the girl in Florida whose pussy you were eatin'."

I picked up my suitcase and walked away. I had only twenty dollars or so, and that wouldn't get me to New York City, which was where I wanted to go. New York had every kind of person. They wouldn't mind one more pussy-eatin' lesbian.

I got to the freeway, put my suitcase on the ground and stuck out my thumb. Cars zoomed by, and soon I wondered if I might have to walk all the way to Manhattan. But then a station wagon pulled to the side and I got in.

A man, woman and two kids checked me out for a moment or two. The man said, "You got balls. A woman by herself—a good-lookin' woman, too—thumbing a ride. I've never seen that before."

"I guess you've never seen a penniless woman before, either," I replied.

They all laughed, and the man said, "I've heard that back in the 'Sixties the world was a much safer place for hitchers, male or female. Today it's different. We're O.K., but you have to be careful about thumbing rides. Never get in with cars that have males only; if they pull over and it's just guys, no girls, wave and say, 'No, thanks.' If it's girls, you know you're safe and they know *they're* safe."

They waved goodbye in New Jersey and I had to keep my thumb out for close to three hours before I got another ride. Finally, someone took pity on me, a male driver, alone and about my age. I figured that if he tried to victimize me, I could probably take him.

"Where to?" he asked.

"Manhattan," I said.

"Let's go." Then, "My name is Wally. What's yours?"

"Darcie Rota."

"Why were you hitching, Darcie? That's pretty risky."

"I hear ya," I told him. "But my options right now are pretty limited. I gave my sob story about being broke and all. He listened and nodded. He was of average size and decent shape; I decided he was harmless. He told me he went to M.I.T. and majored in chemical engineering. He definitely had a half-boner for me but was too polite and reach out and cop a feel. I felt lucky to have gotten a ride from a guy who was mostly a gentleman. All I had to do was listen to him, laugh at his jokes and offer to do the driving whenever he got tired. He said he needed to get back to school as soon as possible, so we didn't have any awkward moment at a motel in which I had to ask him to pay for my room. We yakked away at each other; I learned about the dusty gas model he was working on and I told him some tales about Clarence Darrow, my hero at that moment. Eventually we rolled into Manhattan, and I understand right away that there has never been a city like New York. There I was, in the Big Apple, knowing not a soul and having not a friend.

"Darcie," Wally said, "let me drive you to your front door. I'd feel better about it."

"No, thanks, I'd rather walk. I love walking around Manhattan. I'd appreciate it if you'd drop me by Washington Square." I'd heard that the Square was one of the best places in Manhattan for lesbians. He nodded and pulled over near Washington Square Park. He let me out with his address, a peck on the cheek and a pinch on the thigh. As he pulled away, I wanted to scream, "Wally! Come back! I don't know a fucking soul here! Why don't you transfer to a New York school and be my friend?"

The weather was cold and all I had on was a windbreaker over a sweatshirt. I had only petty cash in my pocket. Alas, the Square was *not* full of friendly, welcoming gay people, so I started up Fifth Avenue and did my best not to cry as I encountered myriad faces, all of them stony and unsmiling. Was this a city or an earthly branch of hell? Whatever it was, it was mine now because I had nowhere else to go.

I got to about 12th Street and panicked as shoppers whisked past me and a few very nearly knocked me on my ass. I wanted to head back towards the Square because things were quieter there. The sky darkened and a drizzle came down that stung my eyes. Wally had given me some speed in the car but it soon wore off and my hunger kicked in. I feared spending money on food. I had no money for a room either, not even at the Hotel Carter, the cheapest flop in Times Square. I decided that I would simply go back to the Square, curl up on a bench—if I could fine an unoccupied one—and freeze to death. My hands hurt from holding my heavy suitcase; my feet felt frostbitten from the socks I wasn't wearing (what need had I for socks in the Sunshine State?). The Square was bare but for some other poor souls who loitered and probably tried not to think about how cold they were. *So, Darcie girl*, I said to myself, *this is another fine mess you've gotten yourself into. What are you gonna do?*

I turned around and stared at the buildings of New York University, although I don't think I knew they were, indeed, NYU buildings. I wondered how I might be able to sneak in there and squat for a night or two. I walked across the street and tried the front-entrance door. Locked. I went to the side entrance; locked, too. Shitfuck. Well, I could always just run around the block all night to keep warm so I would be alive to face the next day—assuming, of course, that I *wanted* to be alive the next day. As I stood there wondering if drowning myself in the Hudson River, I spied a wheel-less old Buick parked at the curb. I thought, *Home, sweet home.*

I went over to the Buick and opened its back door, only to find a long body sprawled across its seat. The owner of the body said, "Good evening, You in need in somewhere to sleep?"

"I certainly am."

"The front seat's free. The steering wheel's been busted and taken out, so it won't get in your way."

"Thanks." I opened the front door, found the space as functional as advertised and crawled in.

Hours later, I woke up to the sensation of being poked in the side. I opened my eyes and saw him, leaning over the front seat. "Hey baby, gotta wake up. Got things to do, people to see. Hear me?"

I got up on one elbow and looked at him. He had big dark eyes, bushy eyebrows, short nappy hair and coffee-colored skin. He looked handsome enough to have chosen *GQ* over homelessness.

"Get up," he said. "There's a coffee shop across the street. I have a friend in there. She'll feed us for free."

I nodded and we traipsed past countless sleepy students as they hurried off to get to their morning classes. We entered the coffee shop, headed for the counter at the back and sat down. A server in a blue uniform smiled at my new friend. "Got a new chick, Girard?"

He smiled back. "Oh, now, you know chicks aren't my thing."

She served us coffee and donuts. I would rather have had ham and eggs, but beggars, as they say, can't be choosers. "Dudes aren't my thing," I told him, "so I guess that makes us even."

Girard laughed. "Where do you come from with that funny accent?"

"A little town called Sundown, in western Canada."

He nodded. "A lesbian from small-town Canada. You spent last night sleeping in an abandoned car. Are you sure your life here is an improvement over your old one in Canada?"

"Guess not. Anyway, is that old car your usual home?"

"No, usually I go to this or that nightclub and let this or that person take me home, keep me warm all night and feed me breakfast afterwards. But I don't know if that would work for you. Lesbians don't do things that way, but I can take you to a couple of dyke bars tonight and they can get a good look at you. You're young and gorgeous, two qualities everyone values."

"I'm not a whore or a freeloader," I told him.

Girard smirked. "So you'll only do it when you're in love?"

"Well, yes."

"Do you want to keep sleeping in that funky old Buick and freeze your ass off?"

"No fuckin' way."

"Then you'd better start making some friends who'll help you out."

Girard spent the day showing me how to jump the turnstiles and ride the subway for free, then he taught me to steal from supermarkets and street vendors. Finally, he introduced me to his "friends"— whores, pimps, pushers, con men. I liked them because they smiled at me and shook my hand.

"Darcie," Girard asked, "what kind of bucks you got?"

"Very little."

"Wanna know how you can make a hundred very fast?" He knew a guy who wished to be whipped and verbally abused. We went to see him; I whipped and swore him; he begged for more, then begged me to stop. Finally he paid me and we left.

"I've decided," Girard told me, "that I'm going to San Francisco. That's the place where I can be as gay as I want to be. Care to join me?"

"I'm tempted, but my inner masochist tells me to tough it out here and see if anything comes of it."

We waited till the coffee shop opened and went to the back counter, where Girard's server friend let us stuff our faces with coffee and donuts. We'd acknowledged to each other that this was a big day for us, and neither of us felt eager to have our big day begin, so we took our time with our goodies until they were in our stomachs and we had nothing left to do but get our butts off those flimsy stools and do what we needed to get done. Outside, we shook hands and went off in opposite directions.

12

Not terribly far from Times Square sat a decrepit apartment nobody else wanted, so I moved in. I had to do my dishes in the bathtub and the wallpaper had peeled half off. Outside I found stained mattress leaning against the building, so I hauled it up and slept on it. My rent, of course, was low by Manhattan standards but high by mine, so I had to get a job soon.

I did just that, serving cheeseburgers and milkshakes at a diner that catered to the after-movie crowd. I felt very hungry most of the time, and while I didn't like eating after strangers, I gobbled up their half-finished platters as soon as they left. I rarely had more than ten dollars in my pocket so I had to be very careful about how I spent it when I went to the bars on the weekend. Sometimes I went to Clementina's, where office flunkies from Jersey went to hook up with flunkies from the Bronx or Brooklyn. Every Saturday night I would lean against Clem's wrought-iron railing and promise myself never to go there again. I had no use for their ego games and power trips, and I hated having to work up the nerve to walk over and ask some woman to dance. Usually, the ones who asked me to dance outweighed the bouncer. I grew bored and frustrated but didn't know what to do about it, so every weekend I came back for more leaning against the railing and staring at the lesbians.

One Friday night someone came along and changed my plans. She came into the restaurant and ordered a strawberry milkshake. Gazing at me, she said, "With a face and body like yours, it's a wonder you can't find a better job."

I swallowed hard. "You speaking to me?"

She nodded. "When does your shift end?"

"Midnight."

"I'll pick you up then."

I smiled. Some gorgeous stranger is taking me home tonight! How awesome is *that*?

She drank her milkshake, went away and came back at midnight.. She shook my hand and told me her name was Molly. She was in her mid-twenties, she'd moved to New York from the Midwest and her only ambition in life was to "be free and be me." Then, "Are they hiring at this joint?"

"Always," I said. "Want to meet the manager?"

Phil, the manager, eyeballed her beautiful boobs and hired her to work with me. We had the same hours and shared a section. She spent all of her money on me, which was O.K. with me if she didn't mind. On our nights off we went to see whichever movie or play looked good. If nothing did, we went for a walk and she kissed me goodnight as she fondled my breasts.

One night we went straight from work to a ritzy nightclub. "We can't go in there," I said. "We need membership cards."

She pulled one out of her pocket.

"Who'd you steal that from?"

"A New York-based actress."

"Doesn't she mind that you have it?"

"Not really. She's my lover."

"No shit?"

"Nope. Does it bother you that I'm a kept woman?"

"No, but it bothers me that I'm not." I added, "If you're so comfy, why do you work at that awful place?"

She shrugged. "Reality check."

"But it's such a shitty job! Why not get a better one?"

"For the moment, it suits me."

"So who's the actress who keeps you so comfy?"

She smirked. "Winnie Kimball."

"Good choice. She's got bucks."

"If you want to meet her, there's a party coming up at Fariel Subedar's. She's a designer, you see. I'll be Win's date, but you can come with us, as long as you're O.K. with my going home with her. I can't wait to see Fariel eyeballing you. She'll come in her pants."

"On that note, let's dance."

We did just that. We danced with each other and with men and women who didn't have partners. They smiled at is, talked to us and invited us to parties. We forgot all about time and at some point noticed that the sky had gotten lighter.

"This city," I said. "It really can be beautiful sometimes. It's after four in the morning and I'm not even tired."

"I'm full of energy, too. My place is close by. Come home with me."

Looks like Darcie's gonna get fucked, I thought.

Her home was big and old and full of expensive furniture. Her big Siamese cat, Moon, mewed at her and hissed at me.

By the time we were in the bedroom, Molly was naked. She was even more beautiful without her clothes on. I stripped and we climbed into bed. She kissed and bit me all over, ran her fingers through my hair and squeezed my butt till I thought I'd scream.

Afterwards, she said to me, "Do you get it on with men, too?"

"Uh, why do you ask?"

"Because," she replied, "I'd hate to think you've ever wasted your good lovin' on a freakin' man."

"Well, I cannot tell a lie. I have been sexual with men; in fact, my first time was with a male. From time I've done it with them, but once I started doing it with women, I thought, 'To hell with men! Women are much more fun!'

"Amen to that," she said, and we made love some more.

That Saturday, I went to Molly's place and met Win Kimball, who looked very much in person as she did on the movie screen. She had beautiful bones and a low, womanly voice. Win seemed very devoted to Molly; her eyes stayed glued to her young lover. Their big cat jumped into Win's lap and she said to me, "Do you like cats?"

"Usually, but not that one. I don't think she likes me, either."

Win nodded. "She has a very nasty disposition. She reminds me of a cat I had when I was a child."

"Where did you grow up?" I asked her.

"On the South Side of Chicago. In other words, a ghetto."

"I grew up in a wretched valley in western Canada, so I guess that makes us even."

"I hope," said Molly, "that neither of you is going to say what a great character-builder poverty is."

I liked Win a great deal. I envied Molly for having the great luck of living with her. If you're going to be a kept woman, you should have someone like Win as your keeper.

"We're about to go to Fariel's," said Molly. "Are you two ready?"

Win and I picked up our coats and put them on. Hers was fine, while mine was cheap and tawdry. I felt ashamed of my indigence and poor clothing, while Win either failed to notice my raggedy attire or was simply above commenting on it.

Fariel lived in a townhouse, and when we arrived, a butler took our coats, which pleased me, although his sneer when I handed him my coat pissed me off. Molly sashayed into the room as Win and I tried to keep up with her. A gorgeous Indian woman with short hair and a big ivory smile came in and kissed Win and Molly. "So glad you could come, dahlinks," she said.

"Of *course* we came," said Molly. "Your party would have been so *empty* without us." Then, "Fariel, I would like you to meet Darcie Rota, our new friend."

Fariel licked her lips as she shook my hand. "So pleased to meet you. Tell me what you want to drink and then we can get to know each other just a little bit better."

"A screwdriver, please."

"Wonderful. Peter, fix this lovely lady a screwdriver. Then, Darcie Rota, you can tell me what you do and are about and all those other things I need and want to know about you. Then we can figure out where to go from there." She chuckled.

"Right now, I keep busy servings burgers and making milkshakes."

"That's what you *do* but that's not who you *are*," Fariel said.

"I want," I told her, "to go to film school."

"Oh? Do you act? You speak with a funny accent. You'll have to do something about that."

"I come from a small town in Canada. I want to direct, but I think I'm lacking something crucial—a penis."

"You don't need one of those ugly, wrinkly things. We'll just have to see what we can do about breaking down those gender barriers in the film industry."

Another woman joined us, and Fariel said to her, "This is Darcie Rota, a Canadian woman who wants to direct American films."

"Good luck with that." The two ladies went away; Molly and Win rejoined me.

"Fariel liked you. She practically came in her pants when she saw you. You're her type," Molly muttered.

"Every woman is her type," added Win.

"I need to go to the ladies' room," said Molly.

"Then go," said Win.

Molly did so, and Win said to me, "Mind if I ask

you a question?"

I shrugged. "Ask."

"Are you fucking Molly?"

"Yes. Got a problem with that?"

"Not at all. She got that job working with you so she could get to know you."

"Why aren't you jealous?"

"I'm too old for that. I want sexual access to her, but if she wants to go down on someone else, too, I'm O.K. with that. Do you love her?"

I shook my head. "I don't love anyone—starting with myself. Anyway, she and I are much too different."

"Really? In what way?"

"Well, she is very impressed by rich people and their wealth. She has too little ambition, while I have too much. She wants to eat well, sleep late and party every night; I want to get into film school and learn to make those movies that I need to share with the world. We have very little in common, but most of the time we can enjoy each other and there's no conflict."

Fariel stole up from behind us. "Have you two been talking about me behind my back? Shame on you."

Above the din, a voice called out, "Fariel! We need you!"

"It's always something." Fariel shrugged. She reached out and squeezed my hand. "Darcie, we won't have the visit I wanted tonight, so let's have lunch next week."

I agreed, and we set a date. She went away, and Win said, "She's going to eat you for lunch, and I mean that literally."

Fariel and I had lunch, and I found it to be terribly awkward. She was as rich as I was poor, so I borrowed some fine clothing to wear and throughout our meal feared slopping food on my temporary finery. Fariel's questions, constant and personal, made me squirm. I minded my manners and did my best to hide my goofy Canadian accent. But I nearly wet my pants when she essentially offered to pay my way through film school if I would move in with her. Fortunately, I got through lunch with only minor pits in that silk blouse and an I'll-think-about-it for Fariel.

On the subway ride back to my dingy excuse for an apartment, I checked out the people who were checking *me* out. I had on expensive, elegant clothes, so my fellow passengers regarded me with admiration and envy. Most of the time, I dressed like a bum because I couldn't afford to do better, so folks looked at me—a tall, dark, beautiful woman just come of age—with an expression like, 'If you look so good, how come you're so poor?'

I wondered what my poor people back in Ontario were thinking and doing just then. I thought of my Sundown people, too, but then decided they weren't my people any longer. What would Reenie and the rest of them think if they could see me on the New York subway, wearing someone else's pretty clothes? What would they think if they knew I'd had lunch with a beautiful, rich Indian who'd said, 'Are you for sale? If so, consider yourself sold'? I'll have to say no; I can't picture myself in her bed every night, stark naked and spread-eagled as she rubs and nibbles my clit till I scream in spite of myself. *Are you my*

whore, Darcie? Yes, Fariel, I am your whore. I know it's a
pisser to turn her down. I would love to let her write
me a few checks so I could go to film school. Her
father provided her with piles of money; why
shouldn't she share some of it with me? How can I
afford film school by myself? The tuition is
outrageous and my job pays chump change. Being
poor sucks ass. I'd have to spread my legs to educate
my brain. Well, I'm not going to do it. Fuck you,
Fariel Subedar, I'm not going to take your money, and
fuck me, Darcie Rota, because I'm going to stay cold
but proud in my crappy little apartment. But isn't
there some way of getting a film-school education
without prostituting myself? Maybe I'm just too damn
proud; my problem is *hubris*. Reenie makes do on
puny pension checks; she refuses to accept anyone's
charity, even welfare. Maybe *hubris* runs in the family.
Family? Hah! What family? All I got from Reenie and
those people was room and board. But wait. If Fariel
loved me, or I her, I would accept her largesse. But in
truth, she didn't give a good goddamn about me; I
was just another piece of ass to her. Shit, I walk down
the street and men look at me like they're coming in
their pants. I walk into a party and Fariel's licking her
lips at my pushed-up tits and heart-shaped ass. She's
not much different from any hardhat at a
construction site; she's just got class and money.

Well, shit, motherfucker, I'm not going to sit
here in this noisy subway train and moan about what
a bad life I have. No fuckin' way. So some beautiful
Indian muff-diver wants to use my pussy for a few
years while she puts me through film school. So I'm
making entire meals of stolen day-old bread and tap
water. Don't sweat it, Darcie. Tomorrow you'll get

your ass over to N.Y.U. and apply for a scholarship. You are the future of American filmmaking and they should consider it an honor to help you to help yourself. Reenie used to like saying that—"Help you to help yourself." I wish I wouldn't think of Reenie quite so often.

13

After months of enduring bureaucratic bullshit, I managed to get a tuition scholarship so that I would be able to take classes in the day and work in the diner at night. Molly disliked our having so little time together. She also thought film school was a joke.

On one insanely busy evening, our little eatery filled up with white, plump, middle-aged theatergoers who grumbled that all the other restaurants had hourlong waits for seating. We worked a half-dozen tables each, and by midnight were stupefied by exhaustion.

As one of Molly's tables emptied, she waved goodbye as she scooped the dollar and change off the table and into her apron. As soon as she set the table, a fortysomething man and his corpulent wife sat there. My guests were stuffing their faces and in need of nothing for the moment, so I stepped away and stretched my tired muscles. Molly dashed past me to the kitchen and came back with a vanilla milkshake and a gigantic banana split, which he delivered to the couple who had just arrived. As she set the banana split before him, he ogled her marvelous breasts.

When he reached up to squeeze one, she jerked backwards, then picked up the big dessert and dumped it over his head. The entire diner burst into a racket of laughter and cheers. The man wiped a handful of syrup and whipped cream off his face, then struggled out of his metal chair, lost his footing and fell on his butt.

He got up, rubbed his backside and took several labored breaths. Then Molly slammed her knee into his testes and he howled in pain. She grabbed a hank of his thinning hair and dragged him into the desired position, then she planted her foot against his buttocks and propelled his big fat body towards the exit.

The manager appeared and said, "There a problem here?"

"Not anymore," said Molly. "This gentleman grabbed my titty, so I taught him some manners."

I stood behind Molly as our boss said, "Sir, are you all right? Molly, you're fired. Get out of here immediately."

When I followed her out the door, he said, "Not you, Darcie. You can stay. Molly's fired."

I put my arm around her and said, "This woman is my wife. If you fire her, you'll have to fire me, too."

Outside, she said, "Come home with me. Stay the night. Fuck me silly."

"Can't do it. I have some major research to do in the morning at the library. Come stay with me at my place."

"But your place is a shithole."

"If you come to my place and spend the night with your face buried in my snatch, you'll forget that it's a shithole."

She sighed. "O.K., but make sure you don't wake me when you leave. You know how much I need my beauty sleep."

When we finally got to my apartment and I opened the door, she made a face. "Yuck! This is just too disgusting. You're a damn fool not to move in with Fariel and let her support you."

I shook my head. "We'll have that conversation another time. I've got enough shit going on in my life at this moment. As glad as I was to see you get back at those creeps in the diner, I sort of *needed* that job because it was my only source of income. Now I need to find another job."

Molly put her hands on her hips. "Shit, Darcie, don't be so fucking proud and stubborn all the time. If you would just hook up with Fariel, that would solve most of your problems. You would live well and study full time at film school. Plus, let's face it, as lesbians go, Fariel is a pretty good catch. You seem to be, like, 'I can't catch a fucking break,' and yet there's Fariel, saying, 'I've got a deal for you right here: Move in with me and study your brains while you let me fuck your brains out.'"

"Fuck off, Molly."

"Witty retort, Rota."

"Let's drop it. You're a kept woman and I'm not because I couldn't do it. Simple as that."

"You're a fuckin' fool. You've spent your whole life in poverty up there in Canada and when someone here offers you a better deal you say, 'Oh, I couldn't move in with her and be her love slave because that would be wrong. Grow up, girlfriend."

"It doesn't have to do with morality or anything

117

else. I has to do with being Darcie Rota, who hates poverty and living in squalor but who has to do things her own way. If you don't understand, fine. Keep living with Win and enjoy your life. But stop telling me I should move in with Fariel, because I'm not about to do that."

"You think you're so superior to me because I'm living with my rich girlfriend and you're not." Then, "Why don't you admit it? You don't love me."

"You're right—I *don't* love you."

"But you sure like licking my bush."

"And *you* seem quite fond of *mine*."

"I wish," she said, "that you would fall in love with me. What's the problem? Don't you like beautiful spoiled brats?"

"Just shut up, O.K.? This conversation is getting too ludicrous."

She hooted. "Want to know what's ludicrous? You are. Your goal is to go to N.Y.U. and get a film degree, then force the whole filmmaking world to do things differently—in other words, to do things *your* way. But the reality is, if you graduate and get that degree, you'll just be another token chick with filmmaking aspirations. Stop being such an idealistic cunt and do the right thing for yourself. Move in with Fariel and enjoy the benefits of upper-class living. That's the best thing you're going to get in this lifetime."

"In other words, move in with Fariel and become her dumb little whore? I have intelligence, and no matter what happens to me, I'll still have my intelligence. So I'll struggle to make do and learn as much as I can about filmmaking, and when my day arrives, I'll make my movies that will allow me to share my visions with the rest of the world. You hear what I'm saying, Molly? Not retarded bullshit Hollywood crap but *my* movies, made my own way. If I'm fifty before I get the money to make my movies, too bad for me, but I'm going to get the money and make those movies. I'm doing it, period."

"I look at you and listen to you and feel shitty about my own life because you have a mission and a purpose and a huge goal to strive for and I don't have any of that."

"Well, too bad for you. Get a life. Get some ambition."

"My parents spoiled me rotten. That's why I have no ambition."

"Bullshit. Plenty of overprivileged kids have highly productive lives full of meaning and purpose."

"Big fuckin' deal. I'm not them, I'm me. What am I going to do, Darcie? Huh? Tell me!"

"Can't do it. You've got to decide these big things for yourself."

"But it's so hard."

"It's always been hard. It's meant to be that way."

"Life shouldn't be hard," she said.

"Well, if it was easy, our successes, when and if they happen, wouldn't mean so much to us."

"I'm sorry if I've offended you during this conversation."

"We'll pretend this conversation didn't happen, if that's what you want."

"I'm sorry I cost you your job tonight," she said.

"I can always find another one."

She nodded. "I gotta go, since it looks like I won't be eating you out tonight. See ya." Presently I

119

watched her walk to the corner and flag down a taxi.

14

I soon got a job as a secretary at Blumenfeld Publishing. I worked with a number of other women at desktop computers, doing very boring work. But I soon caught the attention of my bosses by showing that I could spell my own name, which some of the others could not. The honchos even noticed that I could write breezy copy for book jackets.

Hana Pavolva, the author of many esoteric books, came in one day to check on some matters that concerned her latest book. She trusted no one, so they palmed her off on me. Every other week she and I went over manuscript changes, author photos and whatever else might go wrong. "I love it that you're so meticulous," she said. "Is it true that you're also attending school full time?" Then, "Why don't you have dinner with my family?"

I said yes, and showed up at her brownstone at the requested time. She met me at the door and deposited me an easy chair so that her husband could entertain me. He was a professor of history and looked at me while he talked to himself. Then his daughter, Celia, came in and said hi. She had wonderful almond eyes and a clear, fair complexion. Her breasts were large and naturally jutting; she wore no bra. Her hair, which hung down to her butt, was blonde, red and black in sections.

Hana seemed delighted that her daughter and I immediately got into a conversation. Celia told me that Jimi Hendrix, Janis Joplin, Jim Morrison and Kurt Cobain had died at age twenty-seven. Hana had no idea who such people were and probably wondered why Celia found them so fascinating, as if dying before thirty were something to brag about. Hana spent most of her time mentally living in previous centuries, but when she joined the rest of the world in the present day, I got the feeling that she enjoyed my company.

During dinner she tried to get her husband to make small talk but he just kept eating and frowning. I guessed he had nothing to say. After eating he retreated into his study, to open his books and lose himself in things that interested him.

"Thank you again for your help," Hana said to me. "You're becoming a fine editor."

"I'm not really an editor at all. I'm just doing that for income while I do my real thing."

"Which is what?"

"I'm a film student at N.Y.U."

"Have you made any movies yet?"

"Just a little one. Two minutes. I don't have my own equipment, of course, so I have to borrow theirs. The department is dominated by men who resent a woman's presence, so when I go to check out a piece of equipment for the day, they say, 'Oh, we have nothing available right now. Check back later.'"

Hana frowned. "That's awful. Can't you do

anything about it?"

I shrugged. "I file complaints but nothing ever seems to come of them."

Hana nodded. "And what happens once you graduate? Does your life as a movie director get any easier or better? I doubt it."

After that dinner, we saw each other for evenings out. We saw an especially funny play and, as we strode down the street, she said, "That was so entertaining! It made me want to dance."

"That can be arranged. We can dance together."

Hana frowned. "Where?"

"At a lesbian dance club."

"How do you know about those places?"

"Because," I told her, "I'm a lesbian."

She frowned again. "You don't look like one. Lesbians look and act like men."

"Some do, others don't."

We walked in silence for the longest time. finally, I said, "Does it bother you that I told you I'm a lesbian?"

"Yes," she muttered. "I think I'll just go on home now. If I want to see you again, I'll call you."

15

For about three weeks Hana ignored me, then she called and asked me to see a movie with her. I agreed, and since the cinema was close to my apartment, I said, "Want to have a drink at my place?"

She said yes, I opened my bottle of cheap wine and soon she got buzzed. "Lesbianism freaks me out," she said. "It's not natural or normal." Etc. & etc. "Lesbians should keep their sexuality to themselves" Etc. & etc. Then, "Why are you a lesbian?"

"Because men bore me."

"They bore you! How can that be?"

"They just do. They act like children most of the time. They throw their food and fart at the most inappropriate times."

"You probably just haven't met the right man."

"Or maybe you haven't met the right woman. I'll bet I've gotten it on with more men than you have. They all have the same tool down there and they use it in much the same way. Gets boring after a while."

We paused. "What is so much better about sex with another woman than making love to a man?"

"For one thing, women are much more intense."

"Heterosexual bedroom activity can get pretty intense, too."

"Yes, but it's just that much different with women."

We sat there some more. Hana smacked her lips and looked at her glass. This bitch, I said to myself, cannot hold her booze. "Maybe," I said, "you have a soda instead of more wine. I don't want you to get drunk."

"Oh, I'm O.K."

"Are you?" I liked Hana, and thought her sexy as hell, but she had this thing about judging me because I was a lesbian and that really pissed me off.

"Darcie?"

"Yes?"

"Have you laid many women?"

"Zillions."

"Zillions isn't a number. Be serious."

"Laid and been laid by more than my share. Haven't met a chick yet who could resist me."

Then I put a long, hot kiss on Hana's lips. She tried to break free, then just sort of leaned into it. Afterwards, of course, she insisted that she didn't like it.

"Shame on you, Darcie. You're like a man, inviting me up here and then kissing me, taking advantage of me like that."

"Here, let's try it again." I clutched her shoulders and she grimaced at first, then let the kiss happen and kissed back every bit as passionately. Presently we began playing dueling tongues. Then her homophobic, Puritan side won over and she pushed me away. "How awful of you!" She wiped her mouth.

I smirked. "So sorry if I offended you." Then I pushed her backwards so that she fell onto my mattress. I fell on top of her and we made love.

"Where are we?" she asked.

"In my apartment, of course."

"Not good enough. We're in a men's restroom."

"Really?"

"Yes. We're in the Times Square subway station. We're standing at the urinal."

"Yuck."

"Darcie, I need a fantasy. I can't get off otherwise. So we're standing there and you say to me, 'Nice cock. May I suck it?'"

I cleared my throat. "Nice cock. May I suck it?"

She giggled and spread her legs. "Say some more."

"Like what?"

"Just make something up. The raunchier the better."

"Your cock," I said, "is way too big and beautiful."

"Ask if you can touch it."

"May I touch you big beautiful cock?"

She shuddered. "Oh yes! Kiss it and touch it and suck on it." Her eyes rolled into the back of her head and she trashed around, having one of the most animated orgasms I had ever witnessed.

Panting and sweating, she rolled over and faced me. "Want me to do you now? I don't know how to eat pussy, if that's what you want, but you can tell me how. What's your fantasy?"

"Don't have one."

"Sure you do."

"Nope."

"But who can make love without a fantasy? I'll bet you have one but you think it's too perverted to tell. You can tell me. It'll make me horny all over again."

"No fantasies here. I just like to strip and fuck. It's the kissing and touching that get me turned on. Don't need any talk."

"No wonder you're a fucking lesbian. Anyway, I want to make love to you even if you don't have a fantasy. Are you aware that you're totally gorgeous? Of course you are—all gorgeous women are."

"So, what's my fantasy?"

She did this rap about our being at a boys' school, and soon she had her face between my legs and was wetting me down as if she'd been doing so all her life. Still, I knew our chances for a relationship were slim and zero, and I didn't like her fantasies that had us playing men.

After we fucked, I wanted her to spend the night. I thought it would be nice to wake up as the sun rose and give each other a good-morning hug and kiss. But no; I woke up alone and wondered if I would ever get to screw another straight chick again.

16

I didn't call it quits with Hana immediately. I needed her companionship and conversation—we went to dinner and the theater; she told me about her childhood in Europe. I grew tired of the sex but she pursued it with the increasing exuberance of a child discovering a shiny new plaything. Our carnal relations reached their nadir for me when she said, "I want to piss on you." I told her that I liked her and wanted us to be friends, but being pissed on just wasn't my thing.

"Friends?" she asked. "What's that supposed to mean? I want to expand my sexual horizons and you say something like that!"

"Piss on someone else."

"No. I want *you*." She did and didn't. She felt ashamed of me and had made a point of not introducing me to her friends. She even asked me not to come by her workplace at quitting time so I could walk her home. She probably feared that her colleagues would get the wrong idea about us— meaning they would get the *right* idea about us. Out of loneliness, I stuck around for as long as she would have me. I was the only chick majoring in filmmaking and my classmates were a bunch of guys who resented me for being better at our craft than they were. I had thought that filmmaking might be something open to women, but it turned out that it actually was a boys' club who thought that standing behind a movie camera was an exclusively male enterprise. I went to the bars looking for stimulating conversation and occasionally even found some. But just as often I encountered people at those places who couldn't wait to mention that they knew, or had met, someone worth knowing or meeting. I didn't care about who they knew; I wanted to find out what they knew and what they did. These conceited cuties weren't up to much—they just hung out and did nothing. They mostly just bided their time. But I was damned if I would go back to those dyke bars like Clem's or the Lusty Lady where the diesels flexed their muscles and checked me out as if wondering what kind of underwear I had on. So that left ditzy, daydreaming Hana, apparently the best of all my options.

Celia resolved my issue. The three of us would go out sometimes. I was too freaky for her friends but OK for her daughter. Hana encouraged me to get friendly with Celia, who was closer to my age than Hana was. I didn't give much thought to our ages but Hana kept bringing them up. Celia was only a half-dozen years my junior. She knew that her mother and I were lovers; she thought it just fine. "Do you know," she asked me, "that my mother wants to go to bed with me?"

"Is that so?"

"She won't admit it, of course. I'd like to go for it. She's very sexy. But I'm sure an incestuous thing would really freak her out. Myself, I don't think in terms of taboos. If it feels good, do it."

"I hear that. I have no opinions on incest because the people I called Mum and Dad were not my biological parents, and I've always been very aware of that."

"My mom would do well to lighten up and get comfy with the fact that the sight of my body makes her hot."

"Well, don't try to seduce your mother. She's got other things going on right now."

"Really? What's on her perverted little mind?"

"Not going to tell you. It's a secret."

"Darcie, why do you have to be so discreet?"

"Because I'm destitute."

"How would you feel about wetting *me* down? I'm yours for the asking, you see."

"I don't like easy lays."

"Yes you do. Everyone does."

"Your mum wouldn't like it."

"Well, who the fuck would tell her?"

"Get me one red rose," I told her, "and I'll let you take me to bed."

She nodded and ran down the street. Presently she returned with the item and handed it to me, smiling. We ran off to my decrepit apartment building, stripped naked and flopped onto my sorry excuse for a bed. She shuddered and sighed; she kissed me everywhere and made me scream with delight. She was just being herself, and so was I. Sort of.

Afterwards she said, "We'll have to sneak around if we want to spend as much time as possible together." She and I continued to go out with Hana, and I hated it. One time we went to some art house and as we sat through a foreign double bill with me in the middle, the mum held my hand while her daughter stroked my thigh. The movies bored me shitless, but at the end I applauded as hard as I could just to expend some nervous energy.

Hana seemed to want her mother and me for an all-female *ménage a trois* but at the same time probably felt terrified that it would happen. I was the thing they needed through which to send each other messages. Much of the time I felt lonelier with them than without them.

On one weekend afternoon I sat in Harlem with those two ladies and listened as they ragged on each other as only mothers and daughters can. The mother accused her daughter of acting like a baby, while the daughter accused Mama of getting senile. "I'm not a child, Mother. I'm old enough to be going down on your lover, so deal with it."

"What are you talking about?"

"I'm getting it on with Darcie."

After several moments of gaping, Hana threw a tantrum in a foreign language and then ordered Celia and me out of her life forever. Celia said, "You can't *do* that!" and Hana retorted, "I won't send you to college if you keep eating that slut." Celia agreed, wanting a college education but scarcely willing to work for the tuition money; my pussy didn't mean that much to her.

Soon I yearned to get out of that crazy city with its desperate people. If I had money I could stop fretting over the handful of greenbacks in my wallet and put all my mental energy into making wonderful, disturbing movies. With money, a person is able to protect herself. But getting that money is a very different and more difficult matter. Next year I will graduate and be able to accept full-time employment. Of course, when that happens, nobody will hire me, but I'll try anyway and never give up. Still, I would like to rest sometimes. I want to go back to Sundown a time or two and see the valley I grew up in. Lay my weary body for an afternoon in the meadow and smell the clover. I should try to remember that smell so that it will get me through another winter in this place I've come to call hell. A day in the country would do me so much good; the last time I checked, nobody charged you rent just to lay in the sun.

I thumbed my way to Philadelphia. A hairy truck driver gave me a ride, then started masturbating me as soon as I fell asleep. I slapped his hand away and scowled at him. He minded his manners for the rest of the trip. He let me off at the Greyhound station in Lancaster or somewhere, and after drinking a few Cokes from the vending machine, I boarded the bus that would take me to another station where a second bus would take me a bit closer to Reenie's home in Ontario.

By and by I got to where I was going, although I had to walk a few kilometers. It freaked me out that a few bus rides would take me from the concrete jungle that is Manhattan to the rural wilds of Canada. As I hiked along the road, I fantasized about having a conversation with Bess Lindstrom back in Sundown.

Hello, Bess. Long time, no see. God, you look fifty years old.

"Come on in, Darcie. These are my children."

"Nice for you."

"Son, take your sister outside to play."

"I don't want to. I want to stay here."

"Do as I say."

"No." He pouted and his face turned red.

She smacked him hard on the butt and shoved him out the door. His wails filled the air for fifteen minutes.

"They drive me bonkers but I don't know what I'd do without them," she said.

"I hear ya." In truth, I had no idea why she, or anyone else, wanted children.

"So," she asked, "how come you're back?"

I shrugged. "Just came back for the day, to see if the old country had changed."

"Yeah, Mum told me you'd gone to New York City. Aren't you afraid to live there? Isn't it full of niggers and spicks?"

I said nothing—for what could I say to someone who would say that to me?

"Well," she said, "are you married?"

"No."

"Why not?"

"Don't you remember when we were kids? I said I would never marry."

"Oh, you just haven't met the right man."

"That's because he doesn't exist."

She looked bemused, as if in some weird way my husband-less, childless life were somehow better than hers. "New York City, eh? What are you doing out there?"

"I'm studying at N.Y.U. Film School."

"Are you learning to be a movie star? You're certainly good-looking enough."

"Not me. I'm not interested in being a movie

star. I want to direct big, important films."

"Oh."

"Bess, have you ever thought about that night we spent together?"

She swallowed hard. "Never. Nothing to think about."

"I think about it sometimes. It was one of the better things that happened to me in my childhood."

Bess shook her head. "That was childhood silliness."

"But it happened. Sometimes I can think of that night and I'll just sit and smile."

"It was dumbass shit. I have a family now. I don't have all day to sit around and smile about some stupid crap I did when I was a kid." Then, "You're dressed like a man now. Are you a lezzie still? Is that why you're asking me about some messing around we did years ago? You have movie-star looks and could have plenty of men."

"Are you happy? Do you love your husband?"

"Of course I do. You should find a rich man who will marry you and give you the lifestyle you want."

"Bess, I will never marry."

"Why not? You're young and beautiful, but someday your looks will be gone."

"Gee, too bad for me. I'll worry about being old and ugly when it happens. I'm a woman who loves women. I'm a lesbian, and anyone who doesn't like it can kiss my pussy-eating ass."

"You shouldn't say such things. You're such as smartass."

"Yeah, and when we were kids one night, you sure loved licking my smart-ass."

My fantasy ended and I decided to head back to Manhattan. At least there I could decide my own fate, or labor under the illusion that whatever happened to me was in my own hands.

17

New York City seemed indifferent to me when I got back, but I just thought, Fuck 'em. I decided just to find a place to live, get myself settled in and deal with whatever shit I encountered. The rest of the summer stayed hot and sweaty; autumn felt nice because school started again and I would be a senior, which meant I needed to produce a short film that showed off all the good stuff I'd learned during my four years of study at New York University.

Professor Yount, head of the filmmaking department and a woman-hating son of a bitch, said, "Darcie, what are you going to do for your project?"

"I thought I would do a twenty-minute documentary called *The Soul of Woman in America.*"

"What do you know about that? You're a Canadian!" Sex and violence were fashionable that year. Most of the men were shooting freaky sex scenes intercut with footage of cops beating the shit out of civilians. Not my thing.

"You know that we have limited resources around here. You may have some difficulty getting the camera for a few days at a time. By the way, who will be in your crew?"

"Three of us: Me, myself and I."

"Is that because they have trouble taking orders from a women?"

I shook my head. "It is because they have trouble taking orders, period."

"Well, I'll be eager to see what *The Soul of Woman in America* looks like."

I'll bet you're hoping it looks like a piece of dog shit, I thought.

When I asked to take the camera home with me, they said they had promised it to other students first. So that afternoon I swiped it; I just stuck the sucker into my bag, zipped it and sauntered out, knowing that the people who were responsible for the equipment didn't think I would do such a thing. I had also pilfered as much raw film stock as I could fit into my bag. I went straight to Kennedy Airport and bought a return ticket to Ontario. By that evening, I was in my own house, the one I hadn't visited in a half-dozen years.

"Who dat?" my mother called out.

"It's me. Darcie."

"Darcie!" The door opened and I saw Reenie. She was a sickly shade of yellow and her hair had gone completely white. Her hands trembled as she reached out to grab me and pull me in for a hug. She wept for a moment, then tried to talk but her tongue seemed too big for her mouth. She swayed like a drunkard as she tried to return to her living room. I slipped my hand under her arm and helped her to her reclining easy chair. She made herself comfortable, arranging herself this way and that, and then she looked up at me.

"I s'pose you're surprised to see your old mum after all this time. I guess my sickness had gotten the better of me by now. Can't do much but stare at the TV."

I nodded. "I'm sorry, Mum. I really didn't know you were so badly off."

She shook her head. "You weren't supposed to know. After you left, I decided to keep my complaints to myself." Then, "You didn't give a damn most of the time, anyway. I told Mo, if she ever wrote to you, not to tell you how badly off I was. I can't write anymore because my fingers hurt too much. So, why have you come back? You're not going to get naked with other women in that bedroom, you know."

"Not here for that, Mum. I'm still in school. I've come back to ask you to help me with my schoolwork."

"You want money? I don't have any to give."

"I don't want your money, just your time."

"Why are you still in school? You should be done with that by now. Can't stay in school all your life. Are those American kids too smart for you?"

"I've had to work and make some money so I could pay my bills. That's why it's taking me so long to get through school."

"Well, at least those Americans aren't smarter than you."

"So, will you help me with my schoolwork?"

"That depends. What do I have to do?"

"Just sit right there and talk to me about your life while I film you."

"Film me like a home movie?"

"Yes."

"You got a camera with you?"

"Yes, I got one from school."

"Don't I need fancy clothes and makeup? You need to be gussied up to be in a movie, right?"

"Not for this one. You just need to sit there and tell me about yourself and your life."

"You gonna give me something to read so's I can make a fool of myself and everyone can laugh at me? You used to do that when you were small. Are you gonna do that again?"

"Nope. You just sit nice and comfy and tell me about your life while I film you."

"Who's gonna see it?"

"My professor and classmates. It's for school. I have to do it in order to get a degree."

She scowled. "No! I'm not gonna talk in the movie so's all those hoity-toity New York people can sit there and make fun of me."

"Mum, no one's going to laugh at you unless you tell a joke."

Reenie thought for a moment. "You'll have to feed yourself because I can't afford to keep you while you're here. And don't be havin' no ladyfriends over for the night. I don't like that kind of thing."

"I hear ya." Then, "Where's Big Mouth Annie?"

"Annie? Dead and buried coupla years back. Died from high blood pressure. Doctors gave it some fancy name, but it was what it was. I knew she'd get something like that because she did nothing but worry about things she couldn't control. You want to get sick? That's the way to do it—just try to control your universe. Oh, well. She was good to me and I miss her."

Big Mouth Annie had died. The impossible had happened. I felt sure that even in her grave she was gossiping as much as ever. Reenie said, "We buried her in the boneyard—the one over by the drive-in picture show. It was a very touching ceremony; only thing was, they had that big marquee for the movie theater visible to everyone and the movie they were showin' was somethin' naughty like *Summer's Blonde Booty*. Well, all I can say is I'm glad Annie was dead because if she had seen that marquee she would have dropped dead. She had no tolerance for filth. We buried her in a sleek black casket, almost the very best kind there is, or at least almost the most expensive. You know Annie—'the best' and 'the most expensive' were two ways of saying the same thing. We rode this time in a Cadillac. Wasn't as nice as the car at the last funeral. What car was that?"

"A Lincoln Continental."

Reenie nodded, smiling. "Yeah, that was sure a nice ride. Your father didn't think much of that car. He didn't like Ford cars, period."

"Well, Daddy didn't know shit about cars, anyway."

Reenie laughed and said, "Better go put that stuff in your room before I trip over it and end up in a motorized wheelchair."

I grabbed my junk and hauled it into what had been my girlhood bedroom. Mum had cleared it of all my ribbons and trophies and put a painting of blond Jesus over the bed. I stowed my gear in the closet and went back into the living room.

Reenie rocked back and forth in her recliner like a three-year-old. "Want a cup of tea, sweetie? Or a pop? I always keep lots of pop in the fridge; Roy's little

141

boys sure love that stuff. They're not so small anymore. Roy had to marry her; well, he didn't *have* to but he thought it was the right thing to do. Anyway, they seem as happy as the next couple, so I guess it's worked out all right. Now look at you! Maybe they'll come by now that you're in town for the time being. I don't get out much these days since I sold my car, which I had to do because I needed the money. I'm afraid I can't just live off my good looks. How long did you say you would be here?"

I shrugged. "About a week."

"That's fine so long as you buy your own food."

"How are you getting by, Mum? You don't look fit to work."

"Oh, I manage. I take in ironing or I do babysitting. I get a pension check every month and I don't piss away my money. When I get too old or sick, I'm just going to wander off and let the bears and wolves make a meal of me. You don't have to worry about taking care of me in my dotage."

"If you say so."

"See what I mean? You don't much care about me. You don't send me any letters telling me how life is in New York. I'm sure they have post offices in that big city. I could die out here and you wouldn't even know. You just don't care."

I shook my head. "Mum, I left because you said to me, 'I don't want anything more to do with you.' Also, I did write to you once or twice."

"That was just me being angry. You should have just let my angry words go in one ear and out the other."

"I couldn't do that. You said what you said. You hurt my feelings."

"In one ear and out the other."

"You said I was some bastard child you took in. You said I wasn't your child and you were glad of it."

"Now that's a lie. I've never said any such thing."

"Mum, you *did*."

"Don't be callin' me a bloody liar. You heard me wrong. You were always such a touchy little thing, takin' everything so personal. You and I were talkin' and I said something you didn't like, so you flew out of here and never came back. I didn't call you no bastard child, so don't stand there and tell me that I did. You're my baby and don't ever forget that. Way back when, while I was frettin' over whether or not to take you in, Pastor Niebuhr said, 'She was born to be yours. All children come into this world the same way and the fact that this one's parents aren't married means nothing.' I believed him and still do. I would never call you a bastard to your face or behind your back."

"O.K., Mum."

I went into the kitchen and got her a bottle of pop and some pretzels. I turned on the TV and Mum insisted that I play it loud. We watched game shows; she tried to guess the answers but got most of them wrong. We talked during the commercials and she told me she wished she could get up and dance but her middle ear was so far out of whack that she would just stumble around.

I filmed Reenie throughout the week. At first she got freaked out at the sight of the equipment, but once she sat back in her soft chair and remembered that her job was to do her favorite thing in all the world—talk about herself—she sat back with a smile and flapped her tongue. Whenever she got riled up about something, she would rock harder and talk faster. Once her story ended, she would let her chair stop moving and she'd answer *yes* or *no*. Mum stared with bemusement as I tweaked the camera and made a dozen other adjustments without pausing for a moment, as if she were a medical student watching a top doctor doing brain surgery. But she smiled plenty, too, being the center of attention—*my* attention. She replaced her smile with a frown as she asked, "Why are shooting me from *that* angle? Come closer, but leave enough head room."

When not filming, I did chores for her; I mowed her lawn and ran some errands because her mobility was next to zero. Roy came over with his family; his kids ran around the house while Roy and Mum talked about crap and his wife, Mary Beth, checked me out. She had her hair cut short and colored something like blonde and she wore way too much makeup. "Why do you look like that?" she asked me. "Your clothes look like they've come from the Sally Ann or something."

I tugged at my ancient dark turtleneck. "It *is* from Sally Ann. I couldn't afford anything new. It was either this or go around naked."

Mum laughed. "Yeah, my Darcie, she don't have two nickels to rub together but she can dress as sharp as the next woman." I had been blessed with swarthy, exotic, androgynous beauty, and Mum loved to brag about it. "You'd be a real knockout if you'd start wearing skirts and dresses like a lady."

"But Levi's are so hip!" Mary Beth said.

"And Darcie has the best ass in town," Roy said.

"Just you never mind about Darcie's ass," said Mary Beth. She and Mum left the room, and Roy said,

"Looks like we grew up, eh?"

"Sad but true," I said. "Grow up or die; those were our options."

He nodded. "So you make movies. I can't feature that. Darcie making movies? Naw. I was sure you were gonna be a lawyer, with that yap of yours and your 'I'm gonna win this argument or else' attitude. You were always the smartest kid for miles around. Canada was too small for you. I s'pose I'm dumb. After I got out of the military I came back here and got a job with the city."

"Do you like it?"

He shrugged. "Most of the time. I have a few guys working for me. They're all Natives. They're just like us except for their skin. I would never socialize with them because they work for me—if you socialize with them, they'll think you're friends and forget that *you're* the boss and *they're* not. But they have wives and kids and bills up the ass payable immediately. I learned plenty about life when I was in the service, and it was good to learn there because I didn't know shit when I went in. My dad taught me lots of nonsense and the military straightened my ass out fast enough. I went to Afghanistan. Did you know that?"

I shook my head. "I didn't even know you'd been in the service."

"Well, now you know. I was a changed man when I came back, but I guess my changes were mostly for the better."

"Did you kill anyone there?"

"Nope. They had other guys to do that. I just stood around and tried to look important."

"Well, I'm glad you made it back and you're still mentally together."

"Yeah. Say, mind if I ask you a personal questions?"

"Ask."

"Do you have a boyfriend?"

I glowered. "What do *you* think?"

"Dunno. That's why I asked."

"No, I don't."

"But you've been with men. Not just me. You've been with other guys."

"Yes."

"You're still the only girl I can talk to. The only one who seems to understand."

"But I'm a woman now. A woman is not a girl."

"You've been with girls, too. I know that."

"Well, what of it?"

"Nothing. It's just that we haven't spoken in so long that I just wondered if women were still your thing."

"Most of the time, yes."

He nodded. "It's just as well that you're different from the rest of us here. You didn't belong out here in the boonies. If you had married me or one of the others, you would've just gotten bored and left." He leaned forward and said, "I'm tempted to say, 'Darcie, take me with you back to New York. I'm dying for an adventure, and I'd like to have an adventure before dying.'"

"You need to make sure your family is provided for financially before you run off to have adventures."

Just then the others reappeared.

"Roy," said Mary Beth, "your Aunt Reenie has some pretty new clothes. She sure has good taste."

Roy rolled his eyes. "Nice for her."

"We better get going," said Mary Beth. "Roy, say

goodbye to Darcie. We're gonna drive out and see those new condominiums they're building that nobody can afford."

"Guess we won't see Darcie again for another five or six years," said Roy.

"Unless I drop dead, then she'll have to come back to bury my old bones," said Reenie.

"Oh, I think you'll be around for a few more years," Mary Beth said. She turned to me. "Don't hesitate to write or call once in a while, Darcie. You know our address and phone number."

I nodded. "I'll be in touch."

Presently they were in their beige station wagon, driving away.

"Don't he have a nice family?" Reenie said. "Especially that Mary Beth. She's just the sweetest thing."

"Isn't she, though?"

On my last day in Ontario, Reenie acted like the woman I had always known. She darted about the kitchen, fixing me a substantial breakfast that I assured her was unnecessary. She even made me fresh coffee; she believed that instant coffee didn't deserve to be called coffee.

Then she sat facing me and said, "You've ast me who your real father was. I didn't tell you, but I know that you're so bloody nosy you'll find out sooner or later. Sals had got mixed up with some man from overseas and he was married, so nobody ever said much about it."

"A foreigner? What kind?"

"French, I think. I got to believe he was

handsome because Sals didn't have much use for ugly men. We nearly shit when we found out she was runnin' around with some guy who couldn't even speak English. Neither of them could understand a word of what the other was sayin', but I guess they had other things to do besides talk. That Sals, she had the itchiest pussy of any dame I ever met. Anyway, once he found out she was pregnant, he wanted nothing more to do with her. Liam caught up with him and made him understand that he was never to claim you nor say your were his child. The man just nodded and smiled."

"Did you ever see him?"

"No, but I look at you and figure he's the reason you're so bloody good-looking. You sure look like a froggie, with those big dark eyes. You don't look nothin' like Sals, but you sure have her voice. You been in the States a while now but you've still got your country accent—they probably laugh at you in New York. I can close my eyes and listen to you and convince myself that Sals is talkin' to me. You don't have her body or features or anythin'. You're probably just a younger, female version of your old man. I hear he was a hotshot athlete, traveled around the world and competed. I don't know how he met Sals—she never went near a playin' field in her life. You're a tall, strong girl, so I guess you got most of your looks and strength from him. Sals tripped over her own feet as often as not."

"What was his name?"

"Oh, John-Claude something. It happened a long time ago. It didn't mean that much to me. Sals got knocked up by some frog, he went away and here we are."

"Thanks, Mum. I've always wondered about that."

"Well, I'm not done yet." She stared at me for a few moments, then looked me up and down. "Your birth parents were sure good to you. You have a lovely body. Nice and tall, beautiful titties, great ass, tight tummy. Wasn't so bad myself when I was young. But gravity wins in the end."

"Want some more coffee, Mum?"

"Don't mind if I do. The milk's in the fridge. Milk is gettin' to be as expensive as booze. Maybe I should stop buyin' milk and start puttin' booze in my coffee—probably make me feel better. Burl and I couldn't have kids, you know. He got a disease from some whore and that ended that. I'm tellin' you this because I want you to get the true story right now. You ask other people about this and they'll give you their versions but I'm the one that knows so what I'm tellin' you is the straight-up truth. Bur got a dose from some chippie way back when, and when we started goin' together he started cheatin' on me but I didn't know because I had this way of stayin' ignorant of things I didn't want to know. Pookie, Annie and Jimmy all knew but I didn't. Annie saw him runnin' around with her but wouldn't tell me. Big Mouth Annie managed to keep somethin' to herself! Can you imagine? I coulda punched her out when I learned that she knew but refused to tell me. I s'pose the missus is always the last to know, especially if she don't wanna know and is full of denial. No, I never woulda thunk he was cheatin' on me. He acted the same towards me as always—acted like I was the only thing in the world that mattered to him. Then we went to this party at the Ingles' and I heard all this whispering. I figured they were whispering about me, so I said, 'How come everyone's whispering? If you have something to say to me, say it.' Annie said, 'Well, *someone* should tell her.' I said, 'Tell me what?' Everyone shut up and Pookie hauled Annie into the kitchen. Burl and I went home. I knew something was goin' on. The next day, Pappy came all the way from the other side of the valley to tell me. The people who knew about Burl infidelity thought Pappy should tell me because he was my stepfather and pretty much the only family I had aside from Annie. Pappy told me that my hubby had been seeing a woman named Agnes. He said, 'She's very tall and she acts like her shit don't stink.' I just stood there, not knowin' what to think…especially after what happened to my first husband."

"Your first husband! I thought Burl was, you know, the only one you'd ever been with."

She shook her head, "Nope. Burl was my second. Rupe was my first. He punched me out a bunch of times so I divorced him. He had some girlfriends while he was married to me, and it was quite the scandal when we got divorced. People around here weren't shy about saying, 'Cheatin' is bad but divorcin' is worse.' Around that time I took up cigarettes, too. I'd smoke and blow it into people's faces just to annoy them. I smoked big cigars, too, that smelled like someone farted.

"Anyway, that night I knew I would have to have it out with Burl because he was runnin' around with that woman Agnes. I said, 'What's the deal with this woman?' He said, 'It's true. I been seein' her for a year.' He sat on our sofa, put his head in his hands and cried. 'Reenie,' he said, 'can't a man love more than one woman at a time? 'Cause I can't decide to love you or her. Just both.' That knocked the wind right outa me. *Both* of us? Wasn't *I* enough woman for him? I went to Doc Hanratty and he said to Burl, 'Forget about Agnes. Reenie is your wife; you don't need two women.' So Rupe said, 'Yeah, I hear ya,' and we did reconcile. I forgave him, sort of. But I was a good wife to him and he broke my heart, so I could never forget that. I still don't know how or why he could do such a thing to me." She wiped tears from her cheeks and sat there waiting for me to pat her hand and offer her some words of empathy. Or something.

I sighed. "Mum, all I can say is that I can understand why Rupe did what he did. Some people need more than one lover. They're just not monogamous."

She glowered at me, the daughter who had just told her something she did not wish to hear. "I should have known you would say such a thing. You've got sex on the brain. That's been your problem all your life."

I stared at her, she at me, and we said nothing for a while. I wasn't going to say, "Poor baby, you're the most wronged woman in all of Canada."

She sighed and kept talking, but this time she showed less emotion because I was withholding my pity. "Then you were born," she told me, "and I saw an opportunity. He couldn't give me a baby, but you seemed to be up for grabs. I'd always wanted a baby to dress up and care for. I thought motherhood would make me happy. you became a gorgeous little girl once we fattened you up a bit. They were starving you to death at that Catholic orphanage because they didn't understand that a chubby baby was a happy baby. Rupe said, 'I'm afraid I'll be an unfit father. I don't know what to do.' I said, 'I'll tell you what to do.' He came to love you as much as if you were his own. Of course, in some ways you aren't the daughter I wanted, but you're still mine. All I got in this world.

"You were born to be my baby. That's what the pastor said and he never lies. I raised you to be a lady and did the best I could."

"I hear you, Mum, and I'm grateful. I know you did without so that I could have as much as possible."

She waved me off. "Don't be grateful. A mother is supposed to provide for her child. I did it because I wanted to."

I checked my watch. "My taxi will be here soon."

"When you comin' by again?"

"Not sure. May be a while. I'm pretty busy back there. Besides, money is very tight."

She tsked. "Now, I'll never understand what it is with you and women. A woman isn't going to support you; that's what men are for. I wish you liked men instead of women."

"Well, you married a man and he didn't support you much. You've had to look after yourself all these years."

"Sounds like you're sassing me. I don't care to be sassed. When's your taxi due?"

"Soon. Very soon."

"Well, all I can say now is that I did the best I could for you. This may be the last time we'll be in the same room together. I keep thinking that all the hardships you've had were things we could have avoided if we'd had money. You work too hard, and you're too skinny. You work too hard because you don't have a family fortune to fall back on. Please don't hate me too much."

I put my arms around her and said, "Mum, I've never hated you. We're both very stubborn people and we've had our conflicts. But you've always loved me and I've always loved you."

"And I never said that shit you accused me of sayin'. I never called you a bastard or said you weren't mine."

"I love you, Darcie. You're about the only thing in the world that I care about—you and the TV set."

"I'm glad I mean more to you than that TV set."

We heard the taxi honk and Reenie looked up at me as if big men with guns were coming for us.

"Let me carry your suitcase," she said.

"No, it's much too heavy." I hustled out to the taxi with my suitcase, then headed back into the house for my filmmaking equipment. Then I gave Mum a hug and kiss goodbye.

"Write to me," she said. "Promise?"

"I'll write once each week," I told her.

I sat in the back seat as the taxi rumbled away, thinking that I loved my mother no matter what. My mother, who believed that God made people different colors because He didn't want us to live together. She believed that every woman was only as good as the man who kept her, and that any woman who didn't have a man, or want one, was sick in the head. I liked to think that all kids loved their mothers, and she was the only mother I had ever known. I had always love her, even—especially?—when she made herself very unlovable.

18

Professor Yount's face shriveled up like a scrotum when I walked in with the equipment. He bitched at me about how thoughtless I had been to take all that stuff when so many others needed it, too. He even threatened to strip me of my scholarship, but then realized that I had already used up most of it, so then he went quiet.

Project night was a big thing there. The guys brought their girls and everyone dressed in the shabbiest possible manner, as if looking slovenly were something to strive for and be proud of. I had no boyfriend or girlfriend; I arrived by myself. They got freaked out because I was dateless. Then they turned down the lights and cranked up the projector. The movie everyone applauded most was a Rodney King-esque scene in which some cops haul a black dude out of his car and kick his ass as a rock-music song blares. So many of the student filmmakers nodded and spoke of what a profound bit of cinema that was.

Mine was the last movie we saw that evening. By then, many—most?—of the students had taken off. I thought it rude of them not to stay for mine but tried not to be offended. There was Reenie, simply being herself on camera, sharing her thoughts and feelings about this and that. I had edited it to the best of my ability, and while it lost its momentum now and again, mostly it was twenty minutes of her life, even and logical. My film ended with her saying, "I'm Canadian, but I know my freedom is due to the Americans. Nobody from overseas is gonna come here and invade Canada because America will protect us. So I can just live out my life and die when I'm done. I just hope I still have all my marbles when I go." Fade to black.

Nobody applauded or made a sound as I got up and unthreaded the projector. As these people, my classmates whom I had known for the past few years, filed past me, I shot a glimpse at each one's face but all of them seemed to look away. Presently only Yount and I remained in the room. He tiptoed past me, reached the door, turned to speak to me but said nothing, then left.

I graduated with highest honors but did not attend the ceremony; they mailed my diploma to me. I did not return to the U. or its filmmaking department because I would have felt tempted to brag about my success to the undergraduates who were still plodding along. After my showing, I gathered up my film cans and movie camera and went looking for a job. United Artists said, "Would you be willing to work as a secretary?" Warner Brothers liked my writing and editing skills; they wanted to hire me as a flack who'd bang out PR crap for their movies. They thought it would be terrific if I made coffee, did general gofer shit and made do on a salary that was little more than chump change.

Then I went by and introduced myself to the underground filmmakers. One very famous cult producer/director wanted me to do some-crossing for his next Shakespearean parody. "Beautiful face, great tits," he told me. "I could make you queen of the Bs." Ogilvy and Mather wanted me to work for them as a secretary—"Within a year, you could be shooting TV commercials."

Wow, man!

I found it all highly demoralizing. I'd kept hoping that I would be the token overachieving chick who went straight from college to a job worth taking. Yea for me, right? After all, I was the stud of my class; shouldn't that have meant *something*? I spent those frustrating days pissing away my lunch hours on job interviews, then sitting in the office while Monda inundated me with stories about Mister Blume's man-problems, dreadful days when I edited technical documents that bored me so much that I felt tempted to put my foot through the computer screen. My bad feelings were reflected in the news—I encountered countless stories about people my age marching or racing down streets in protest of the outrage of the day. Alas, I knew that my rage wasn't theirs and that they would have soon kicked me out of their movement for being a dyke. I knew that women's groups were starting up everywhere but that I wasn't their kind of woman. What the fuck! Sometimes I wished I could be a kid again, charging money for glimpses at a boy's dick. I wished I could get up every morning and look at the day the way I had as a child, wide-eyed with exuberance. I wished I could walk down any street without hearing the deep voices of males. Mostly, I wished the whole world would back the fuck off and just let me be Darcie Rota. But I knew better than to expect any of those things to happen. All I could do was make my films, and be such an unstoppable filmmaker that the next generation of filmmakers—dykes or otherwise—could make their flicks without worrying about the obstacles I'd knocked down for them. I have a dozen movies I need to make and I don't want to fight like a tiger till I'm fifty just to be able to make them. But if I have to fight, I'm going to be the meanest, toughest bitch the American film industry has ever seen.